"One of the most power[ ]
in the genre...Lebbon[ ]
contemporary realism of [ ]
of Ray Bradbury."

— Fangoria

"Lebbon is among the most inventive and Original contemporary writers of the dark fantastic"
— Ramsey Campbell, author of *The Grin of the Dark*

"Tim Lebbon is a master of fantasy and horror, and his visions make for disturbing and compelling reading."
— Douglas Clegg, author of *The Priest of Blood*

"Lebbon creates vivid and convincing major and minor characters, places and creatures, blending wonder and nightmare"

— Publishers Weekly

"Lebbon gradually, deftly builds the tension until it explodes in an exciting climax."

— Booklist

"Tim Lebbon is one of the most exciting and original talents on the horror scene. His lean, compassionate stories have a habit of exploding in your face on the very last page."

— Graham Jo~   of
How To Mak~ ~s

11x 5/18

BAR NONE

A NOVEL OF CHILLING SUSPENSE, APOCALYPTIC BEAUTY, AND FINE ALES

Other Books by Tim Lebbon

Novels
The Map of Moments (with Christopher Golden)
Mind the Gap (with Christopher Golden)
Fallen
The Everlasting
Dawn
Berserk
Dusk
Desolation
Until She Sleeps
Face
The Nature of Balance
Hush (with Gavin Williams)
Mesmer

Novellas
The Reach of Children
A Whisper of Southern Lights
Pieces of Hate
Changing of Faces
Dead Man's Hand
Naming of Parts
Exorcising Angels (with Simon Clark)
White

Collections
After the War
Fears Unnamed
White, and Other Tales of Ruin
As the Sun Goes Down
Faith in the Flesh

BAR NONE

A NOVEL OF CHILLING SUSPENSE, APOCALYPTIC
BEAUTY, AND FINE ALES

TIM LEBBON

NIGHT SHADE BOOKS · SAN FRANCISCO

Printed in Canada

First Edition

ISBN: 978-1-59780-097-6

Night Shade Books
Please visit us on the web at
http://www.nightshadebooks.com

For Mum
and all the great memories

With eternal thanks to Jason and Jeremy

ONE

ABBOT

Six months after the end of the world, the air up here is amazingly clear. If I close my eyes I can smell spring on the breeze, and new rose blossoms, and the tang of the distant sea, and if I open them I believe I might be able to see forever. So I keep my eyes closed for a while, trying to isolate a different scent with every breath. Forever is no longer very far away.

Sometimes, when the weather is just right, I stare through rainbows and believe the world is still alive.

I smile at the meaty aroma of turned soil. Jessica is down there in our garden, preparing to plant the seedlings she found in the greenhouse. They were almost dead when we congregated here; drooping and pale, they resembled our own condition, but water brought us all around. I never believed there was any good left in those insipid green shoots, but Jessica is determined, and Cordell says to let her plant them if she wants to. His voice is dismissive, but

1

I see the hope of greenness deep in his eyes.

I stopped to talk to her on my way up here, as I do most mornings. And as is the case most mornings, she looked refreshed from sleep and ready to tackle another day, while my eyes were puffy from crying and grief was a stone in my heart.

"Do you think they'll grow?" I asked.

Jessica shrugged, clapping her hands and sending dirt spraying.

"I dreamed of my wife last night," I said.

Jessica sighed. "I'm sorry."

"Don't be. It's still raw, even after six months. I think it always will be."

She looked at me evenly, eyes giving nothing away.

"You know I'm here to talk," I said, as I had a thousand times before. I was still desperate to discover hidden depths to Jessica's apparent lack of grief.

"I'm fine," she said, as she had responded as many times. "I had nothing to lose, so I can't see this as the end."

"I wish I were you," I said, and Jessica grinned. She startled and shocked me in equal measures.

I breathe in again, enjoying the smell. It reminds me of long childhood summers working on the gardens of the many new houses my parents seemed to have. Whichever place we moved to they wanted to change, and we always seemed to move in the summer, and they always preferred hacking down bushes and planting new shrubs and vegetables than stripping wallpaper and painting doorframes already hidden by decades of successive tastes. They would allocate me a particular corner as my own. I would clear it of weeds, turn the ground, pick out grass roots and the thicker cores of long-dead bushes, and then my own planting would begin. My own planting...

My memory leaches colour and fades to grey. I frown, unable to recall which had been my favourite plant. A flower? A tomato plant? A vegetable, and if so which one, and why?

I open my eyes, disturbed by the fragmenting of the memory. I need a drink.

Jessica believes that the air seems cleaner because we are eating better than we ever had before the end of the world. She says it boosts our senses. We're eating basic, that's for sure. I'm thinner than I've been since I was thirty, and I feel fitter than ever. Cordell is more pragmatic, attributing the clearer air to the sudden lack of pollutants being pumped into it, day and night, by the abusive humanity. *Six hundred million cars fall silent*, he says, *and the world can breathe again.*

I think it's a bit of both, and something more. Our diet is fine, and the air is purer than I have ever seen, no longer brown and hazy above the dead city to the south. No rumble of cars, no grumble of jets cruising the stratosphere, no violent expunging of fumes from skeletal factories. But I think more than anything, our changed perception is down to the drink.

I look out from the tower. A couple of hundred meters down the hillside sits the Manor, an old grey stone building that was once home to a famous architect. I've forgotten his name—I always do, no matter how often Jessica reminds me—but I know that three hundred years ago this tower was his folly. He built it to the love of his life, and doubtless brought her up here on days like today, impressing her with the view, the air, his richness of taste. I suspect he told her he loved her. "I love you," I say to the breeze, and for the first time in a couple of weeks I smell the dead city.

I frown. We all knew this time would come. Cordell maintains that most of the corpses will have rotted away by now, and that the stink of their continuing decay will be an undercurrent to the summer breeze, nothing more. But Cordell has lost no one, or so he keeps telling us. *I was my own man, and I still am, and that's why I'm strong enough to survive this.*

I think Cordell's a fool. If he really is his own man, why has he remained here with us for six months? And really, I can't believe he thinks survival is even an issue. It's obvious that this is the end.

I breathe in again and the scent has gone, but it was there for sure. "I love you," I say again, mimicking that long-dead architect's exhortations to his lady love. Now I smell turned earth, young blossom, water from the stream running around the base of the hill. No death; no corruption. I hope the tower likes the feel of my words across its stone, words it might not have heard for a long time. When we came to the Manor six months before, its owners had fled.

I wonder where they are now. Where they lie; where they rot.

"Time to go back down," I say. Nobody answers me. I've always been comfortable in my own company.

I circle down through the tower and emerge at its base,

pausing to look at the graffiti that decorates the outside of its heavy oaken door. The words are mostly modern. They are the first lines of the first book written about the end of our world, and I promise myself that one day I will come here with a pen and paper, write them down, keep them safe. One day.

Mark S—I'm trying to get to Mother's in the grey. Hope to see you there? I wonder about Mark S, and what the grey is, and why whoever had left him this message found reason to end it with a question mark, as though unsure whether or not Mark S would even want to meet him or her at all. It has been carved into the door and then written over with indelible ink. A message designed to last for a long time. Sometimes I expect Mark S to emerge from the city and crawl up the hillside, but after six months I guess he's either made it to Mother's, or not.

I fucked Lucy on top of the tower. A stamp of ownership by the last habitants of the Manor? Or an expression of bravery and daring by some teenager who had managed to infiltrate the Manor's gardens, climb the tower, fuck the equally daring Lucy atop that old architect's folly? I do not know, and running my fingers over the fading ink tells me no more. Sometimes when I'm up there—I climb the tower a lot, and the others always leave me alone—I walk around the uppermost balcony and try to guess which view Lucy had been taking in, whilst taking in the writer. I cannot even consider that perhaps she was looking inward when the event took place. There is so much to see, and surely after climbing over a hundred steps she would want to appreciate the panorama?

David, Warren, Diane—there's moor than you can ever

dream. I'm gong to find it. Trust in me and I'll be bak.
This was almost fresh when I first arrived at the Manor.
If I pressed my nose to the oak, I could still smell the
chemicals from the ink. David, Warren and Diane have
not joined the rest of us here, but sometimes I wonder
whether one of the others—Cordell, perhaps, or the
Irishman who refuses to tell us his name—may be the
writer. I have yet to work up the courage to ask any of
them. I'm not sure what dissuades me, but I think it's the
hope that there's still something out there other than us.
The hope that this writer, unable to spell but determined
to find more than the others could ever dream about, is
still searching the dead landscape. Maybe one day they'll
find a truth. Maybe one day they'll return.

There's a wide swathe of daffodils around the base
of the tower. They are mixed into yellows and creams,
and the bulb species must have been varied to give a
solid eight weeks of blooms. Old flowers are brown
and fading, whilst new ones shine through. I kneel and
cup one bloom, staring at its random perfection, and
I try to remember my wife's face. I close my eyes, but
there is a shadow blocking her out. All I can recall is
the knowledge of her tears and pain as the plagues took
her away. "Ashley?" I ask. Still only her tears, and my
memory's response is her angered cry as she felt herself
slipping away.

I definitely need a drink. There's not much left, but
that has not prevented us all from drinking every day.
Temperance has died with the rest of the world.

I stand, stretch, and realise that something is very, very
different.

Jessica is still digging in the garden, sheltered from the heat in the Manor's shadow, comfortable in her own strange acceptance of everything that has happened. Cordell is somewhere out of sight, perhaps talking with Jacqueline in the massive dining room. The Irishman is sitting on the tree swing hanging from the big oak tree beside the Manor's driveway. He's smoking. He is always smoking. He never smokes in the house, because he says he respects our health. Cordell always laughs at that, but each time the Irishman says it, I get a lump in my throat.

I look beyond the Manor, along the driveway, past the boundary hedging, down the wooded hillside toward the river and the dead city beyond. Though I'm no longer up in the tower I can still just see over the Manor's rooftop, the river a silver snake in the distance, the city a smudge of stillness beyond. We've seen many animals in the six months we've been here, some of which we can't quite explain, but nothing has ever moved in the city. Above it, yes—those flying things. But its streets are always still and silent.

But now something is different, though I can't yet see what. I close my eyes and breathe in, thinking that perhaps I have smelled a change on the breeze. There's another whiff of rot and my eyes open. *Yes, but I've smelled that before,* I think. *We all have. We know it's there, we know the city is filled with dead people. However much we try to forget that, we're not stupid. We've always known that the winds would turn to come from the south when spring heats into summer.*

That's not the change. Disturbing though it is, the

smell is nothing new. Even in the winter just passed, when heavy snow would have marooned us here had we not already been committed to staying, we sometimes awoke to the smell of decay.

I hold my breath and listen. Jessica is singing, her voice a bare whisper, words lost to distance. The tree swing is probably squeaking beneath the weight of the Irishman. Birds call from the trees, a breeze hushes the leaves, crickets scratch at the air from the grasses growing long across the hillside... and there is something else.

I concentrate, trying to separate the myriad sounds I know from the single sound I do not. Its strangeness confuses me for a while, as though the length of time since I have heard a noise like this has wiped it from memory and planted it deep in my drunken dreams.

I turn and start running back up the tower's curving staircase.

By the time I reach the top balcony I am out of breath. My heart is hammering at my chest, and I'm afraid that I will have a heart attack and tumble back down. I try to think of Ashley, but once again it is only her pain and tears I can recall, the rest of her—our past, our life, our love together—overshadowed by the end of the world. I know that she was beautiful, but it is a certainty rather than a memory. I hope she would smile to calm me down, and that hope calms me, and I look south toward the city.

I cannot guess how I heard the motorbike from so far away. Even now, three or four minutes after first detecting the growl of its motor, it is only just visible on the long road that leads from the river bridge junction deep into the rotten heart of that place. I shield my eyes from the sun and watch the black speck weaving between abandoned cars, buses and vans. I can hear the rise and fall of its motor as it speeds and slows, passing from view behind an overturned army truck, appearing again, and now I can make out that the rider is wearing no helmet.

Why bother? Cordell would say.

Because there are so few of us left, the Irishman would reply.

The bike clears the last of the cars and passes the few buildings on the other side of the river; the Royal Oak, the expensive apartments, the boys' school that has been closed for a decade. The bridge is clear. For some reason no vehicles were left there. The bike powers our way, and as it speeds up its motor seems to echo from the whole hillside.

Still a mile away, I think, *road to climb, the lane to navigate, then the gravel driveway. But it feels as though it's here already.*

"Jess!" I shout. Jessica looks up from her planting. "Someone's coming out of the city!" I see her stand, arms limp by her sides, and then she drops her trowel and hurries into the Manor's kitchen.

The Irishman jumps from the tree swing and looks my way. "Who?" he shouts, cupping his hands to his mouth. For now his voice drowns the sound of the motorbike, and for that I am grateful. Within minutes that will no longer be the case.

"Guy on a bike!" I shout. "I'm coming down." He nods, waves and runs for the Manor.

I start down the staircase for the second time in ten minutes. I'm painfully alone. It's a feeling that has hit me often since the plagues came and went, but lately it has happened less and less. I'm not sure whether that's because I'm adapting to being alone, or because we are forming some sort of tentative family here. Distant, cautious, often unwilling, but a family nonetheless. A family of survivors.

They'll all be in the dining room by now. Cordell will be handing out the guns while the Irishman tries to calm their fears, telling them that this could be a survivor from another part of the country. They'll be scared, but excited as well. We haven't seen or heard from anyone else for over four months. Jacqueline will whisper something that no one will hear, and Jessica will be strong and impassive, shaking her head at the Irishman's passionate pleas, offering a dismissive smile to Cordell as he predicts trouble. She seems to be stronger than all of us, but once I thought I heard her crying herself to sleep.

I need a drink now.

Perhaps that's why the motorcycle man is coming.

Maybe he knows.

As I run, I pull out my flask. The beer is warm and flat, but I pause and gulp it down. I'm nervous. I need some taste of the comfort in times gone by. For a minute or two, I need to go away.

I remember drinking Greene King Abbot Ale on the banks of the Usk, relishing its hoppy crispness, its sweet caramel aroma and nutty aftertaste, admiring the slight head that stuck to the glass, and I was halfway through my third pint when I saw her. At first I had to shield my eyes from the sun to make out whether or not she was real. She had crossed the river bridge, a mirage emerging from the blazing heat, and now the sun battered down behind her and threw her melting shadow my way. Where it touched, my skin grew warmer. The sun was so powerful that it shone through as well as around her, curling across curves, piercing hair and eyes and meeting again before her, holding her, almost wiping her from existence. I squinted, trying to form a shadow for my eyes. She ran her hands through her hair and made a sunburst halo. Then she sighed.

I had still not seen her properly, but I fell in love with that sigh. Perhaps it was the beer in me—three cool pints on such a hot day, and I had not eaten since a token slice of toast for breakfast. The Abbot lay light on my stomach and heavy in my veins, giving the sun more power, sensitising my eyes to the brightness and heat, and this miracle vision before me.

I took another swig of beer, draining my glass. Smacked my lips. God, I loved beer. There was something so intensely powerful about that taste, and yet so primal, as though with each fresh mouthful I was blinking back to the early history of myself, a potential that could not even shift a speck of dust in those ancient African plains where humanity was born. Sometimes I had moments when I thought the truth of things was so very close to my lips, just a whisper away. The feeling would last forever—a second, maybe two—and then I would speak, and I always said the wrong thing. I used to wonder whether I was the only person this happened to, but sitting on that riverbank with an empty glass warming in my hand, I shifted to the side just enough to see her face. And I knew then that it was not only me. We all have the potential of truth and revelation within us. I saw the way her whole body paused, as though the world held its breath on her account, and then her hand went to her cheek, fingertips tracing the smooth skin.

"Don't speak," I said. I knew that she heard me, though she showed no sign. "You'll never say the right thing."

After a dozen rapid heartbeats Ashley turned and stared at me. The sun allowed us that contact now, still hot, still blazing the ground dry, but permitting us to see each other without its interrupting glare. "I had a moment, but it's gone. That's okay. I like mysteries. Can I buy you a drink?"

I smiled and held out my glass.

She sniffed the empty glass, closed her eyes. "Abbot."

And there was no way I could ever fall out of love again.

TWO

OLD PECULIER

I am exhausted. I've had more exercise since the plagues than in the two decades preceding that catastrophe, but I am still on the wrong side of forty, and my body is far less forgiving than it once was. My legs are burning from running up and down the tower, and as I stumble down the steep path my shins feel as though they're being sliced with a blunt knife.

I can hear the motorcycle engine above my laboured breathing. It is close, probably approaching the long, overgrown lane that leads eventually to the Manor's gravel path. Three minutes away? Two?

Jessica appears at the Manor's rear door, gesturing with her hand. "Come on!" she shouts. I can see the Irishman behind her, face clouded by concern. There is no sign of Cordell. Probably at one of the front windows with our shotgun.

"Coming as fast as I can!" I say. I run past the pond

built into a terrace in the hillside, sent on my way by several splashes as things jump back in. The wildlife here is diverse and fascinating, and I have spent long, spring afternoons sitting by the pond drinking ale. It seems to be a good venue for my memories.

I keep glancing at the long curving driveway that leads to the entrance between rows of old trees. We never bothered closing the cast iron gates, even though Cordell suggested it several times. *Why bother? There's no one else*, Jacqueline whispered. Now I wish we had listened to him. *Just in case*, Cordell said. *Easy enough to open them if and when we do need to leave, and they're strong. They'd withstand…* But no one wanted to hear any more. *Withstand a lorry ramming them*, he said. We all remembered those final days of martial law and curfew, NBC-suited soldiers shooting any civilians who dared sneeze or hold their heads, the Prime Minister on TV telling us why he'd had to nuke London, the mass graves, the burning. And we all wanted to think that was in the past.

As I pass into the shadow of the Manor—warm to cool, as though someone now stands between me and the sun—something appears between the huge stone gate posts. The motorbike roars, and gravel sprays behind it like heavy rain.

I run past Jessica, offering her a smile. It does not cool her frown. "Cordell!" I shout. I know he'll be the one most likely to open fire first.

"He's in the front room," the Irishman says. He's standing out in the hallway beyond the kitchen, worrying at a loose quarry tile with his heavy boots. He has a knife strapped to his belt, but his hand strays nowhere close.

I run past him and pelt into the living room. It stinks of old books. "Cordell!" I say again, pausing, leaning over and resting my hands on my knees. I look up and see him standing by the window, shotgun resting in the crook of his left arm.

"One man on a bike," he says. "Not wearing a helmet. Long blonde hair." He glances back briefly, and I'm comforted by the control in his eyes. He's not likely to blow the man from his bike without provocation.

"Jacqueline?" I ask.

"In the sitting room. She's got the .22."

I nod. The air rifle is an old single shot model, primed by pumping the barrel. We use it for hunting pigeons and ducks, and none of us are a very good shot. If she does use it, she'll have to get him in the eye to cause any real damage.

"I've told her to follow my lead." Cordell sees my concern, hears it in my laboured breathing.

The bike circles the dry fountain in front of the Manor. The rider takes it slow, showing that he is not a threat, and also that he's unafraid. His hair is indeed long and blonde, tied back in several places with what look like metal bands. He rides in shirtsleeves, and his heavy forearms are dark with exposure to the sun, ridged with prominent veins. No tattoos. No piercings that I can see. No sunglasses. It's an old model motorbike, a real antique, and I find the grumbling engine strangely comforting. Everything is very quiet nowadays. It's good to hear this. It's almost normal, and yet this man is so far from normal that I feel cold.

"What is it?" I ask, and my strange wording provokes no comment from Cordell.

We stand together and watch the biker come to a halt. He silences the bike and kicks down its stand. Then he dismounts, stretches, twists the discomfort from his back, yawns, and turns to look at the Manor for the first time.

We lock eyes. He knows exactly where we are, and he probably knew the second he drove in between the open gates.

Maybe he saw me seeing him from the tower, I think, but it's a crazy idea. He'd been a mile away at least, and I was the one hidden away.

"He's looking right at me," Cordell says, and from across the hallway I hear Jacqueline gasp out loud.

"Where's he been?" I say. "I thought we were the only ones."

"We've talked about that," Cordell says, and we have. About how we cannot be the only ones left, how there must be other survivors, why we did not die, why we were spared. And yet we have heard or seen nothing on the airwaves for months, no sign of life from the dead city beyond the river, and the sky is clear and blue, unhazed by smoke or the exhaust from aircraft. The idea that we're the last ones left is faintly ridiculous, but much of the time it's also the only thing I can believe.

If there are others, why haven't we met them by now?

"He's not one of *them*," I say. "One of those flying things. From above the city."

"I've never seen them." He's sticking to his usual story, though I'm certain he's lying.

The man approaches the front door and I hear

Jacqueline dash into the hall. I rush out to be with her—I can never quite tell what mood she's in, how dangerous she can be—but she is already reaching for the door locks. Jessica stands just behind her, and the Irishman is back in the shadows beneath the staircase. The most optimistic of all of us, he seems to be the most afraid.

Jacqueline has left the air rifle leaning against the timber wall panelling and I snatch it up. *It wouldn't do any good*, I think, but I try to ignore the idea.

Cordell is beside me, still cradling the shotgun.

"Do you really think we should do that?" the Irishman whispers from under the stairs, and the door opens inward.

The man stands there for a while, letting the sun spill in around him. His shadow leans out before him, stretching across the timber floor and pooling around my feet. He smiles. "Afternoon," he says. "Any chance of a beer?"

"Who are you?" Jessica says. There is no trace of threat or fear in her voice.

"My name's Michael," the man says. "At least, it is today."

"Just today?" I ask. He looks at me and his attention is intense.

"I left it behind six months ago," the man says. "When I need to feel as though I still belong to the past, I give myself a new name. Today, it's Michael. If you'll humour me—listen to something I have to tell you all—perhaps it'll stay Michael for a day or two longer. I hope so." He glances down at the floor as though staring at his own shadow. "I'm tired of being lost."

"That beer," Jessica says. "We have some. Not much.

Not much left at all, and we don't like to…"

Michael nods. "I know what you mean. I've been into some places, and it's stealing from the dead. It tastes bad. And it's all going off."

"All of it?"

"Everything. All bad."

"You just rode out of the city," I say. "I saw you."

He nods. "You have a good memory," he says, and for some reason I know he's thinking of Ashley.

I shift nervously, shifting the air rifle. It slips along my arm and feels cold all over again. *But I don't,* I think. *I have no memory. Only her pain, and her tears. I can't see her unless I drink, and that's no way to be.*

"What were you doing down there?" Cordell asks.

"Holding my breath. It's good to breathe again."

"You're scaring me," Jacqueline whispers. Jessica reaches out and touches her shoulder.

"I'm sorry," Michael says. "This is all so strange. I haven't spoken to anyone for a long time."

"Where have you been?" I ask. "Is there anyone else? Are we the only ones? How did you know we were here?"

Michael smiles and steps forward, entering the Manor uninvited. "Any chance of that beer, and we can have a good long chat?"

I glance at Cordell, then turn and look at the others. None of us says anything, but in that silence the decision is made. "Of course," I say. "And you must be hungry."

Michael's eyes widen and he touches his stomach. "Ravenous."

We've talked about the things we occasionally see above

the city, floating there in warm currents, sometimes dipping down and rising again with something dark and vague clasped in their claws, or feet, or whatever they have. We all seem to see something slightly different, and Cordell claims to see nothing at all. My impression is of small, winged people, flying with staccato movements like something from a Ray Harryhausen animation. Jacqueline sees large birds, Jessica sees moths, and the Irishman says he sees only shadows, drifting up and down like whiffs of smoke or ash from some distant, unseen fire.

We don't know what they are, or where they come from, or what they're doing. But they seem relatively harmless. And sometimes I think they're ghosts, projected there by each of us because we cannot bear seeing the city so still and silent.

Michael does not resemble anything we have seen. I step back as he enters. His shadow passes over my legs just before Jacqueline closes the door, but I feel nothing.

We take him into the dining room and he makes himself at home. Sits, sighs, looks around. He is confident, but there's also an underlying gratitude, a look here and there that says, *I am so glad I found you all.* Perhaps the confidence is a front, but I think not. We all handle survival in our own way, and it seems to me that Michael thinks he is one of the lucky ones.

Cordell and Jessica make dinner, though neither of them stays out of the room for more than a couple of minutes at a time. They don't want to miss anything. We all appreciate that, and while they cook we talk about the Manor, what it was like when we found it, how we managed to stock some food and drink before the plagues hit their worst. None of us mentions how low the stock is running, and though Jessica talks at length about the gardens and how much food she is planting, we all know that it can never be enough.

"So who's in charge?" Michael asks. He looks at me, then away again. Glances at Jessica. His gaze rests on Cordell.

"None of us," Jacqueline says. "We make our decisions as a group. There are stronger ones, and... those of us not so strong. But we're all survivors together."

"Yes," Michael says, looking at his hands in his lap. His fingers are entwined. "That's good to hear."

Jessica comes in from the kitchen. "Almost ready," she says. We take our seats around the table, and I wonder whether Michael will expect one of us to say grace.

Cordell and Jessica bring in the food, several steaming pots of vegetables and hot dog sausages with fried onions and mushrooms. The smell is mouth watering, and Michael's eyes go wide. "You really are surviving here," he says.

"We're doing more than that," I say. I look at Cordell and he nods. "Excuse me for a few moments." I leave the dining room and breathe a sigh of relief when I'm on my own once again.

The hallway is quiet, and now that the sun is sinking the shadows stretch out, friendly shapes that I have come to know well over the past few months. *You really are surviving here*, Michael said, and he is right. But I am also remembering. That is what my survival is for me, a process of recollecting and honouring, of creating my life with Ashley over and over again.

I seem to have forgotten so much over such a short space of time, and digging for the memories makes me feel more and more guilty. I still cry, but it's at the idea of my dead wife rather than a particular thought. Walking the gardens, listening to nature, I see and hear only her final moments of pain. Everything else is shadow.

But with a drink in my hand, things change.

I pick up the big torch and go down into the cellar. It's as large as the footprint of the mansion, split into several rooms that are mostly filled with rotten furniture and other junk. But the first room is different, and it's the only one we use. When we congregated here it was fully stocked with dozens of ales and wines, and after that first week it played a big part in our decision to stay. There isn't much left now, but I bring up a crate of the good stuff, a selection of bottles that fills me with an ache of nostalgia and the thrill of knowing that I will soon be remembering Ashley.

I hurry back upstairs, and as I walk into the dining room the subdued chatter ceases.

"I do hope you're not a lager drinker," I say. Michael eyes the bottles as I place them on the table, and grins.

We eat the meal, and drink, and the chat comes easily. He tells us something of where he has been and what he has seen, but for some reason that seems unimportant. As darkness falls outside we move from the dining room to the living room, and Cordell ventures to the basement for more beer. We are all drinking, though we know that supplies are running low. None of us has yet dared voice the fear of what may happen when we run out. I can barely think beyond that day, and I'm sure it is the same for everyone. Beer is our drug, our life, and for many of us our saviour.

Michael seems unconcerned. He says that there is much more of everything. There's something about his eyes that makes me think there's a distance there, some defence—intentional or not—that means he's slightly removed from what he's saying, and how we respond.

Once, I see his eyes turn watery. He looks down at his hands and blinks rapidly for a second or two, as if trying to dislodge a speck of grit. He blinks the tears away.

Relaxing in one of the wide, soft chairs that make the living room our favourite place in the Manor, Michael is the centre of attention and the odd one out. He tells us about how he found the old motorbike idling by the side of the road, petrol tank half-full, and how he turned it off and spent the next six hours searching for its owner. The ditches on either side of the road were empty, as were the fields, and although he found six bodies in a farm building half a mile distant, they were all old and decayed. "And there were fat rats," he says. "Dead cows, skeletal chickens, fat rats."

Someone pops another lid from a bottle of beer, and that metallic snick becomes the mark between one conversation and the next.

Michael mentions that he has seen other people. I pause with a bottle half-raised to my lips. "But they're not like you," he says.

"How do you mean?" I ask. The fire crackles, and a log

spits as a bubble of sap explodes. Jacqueline, sitting close to the fire so that there are no shadows about her, reaches out one lazy foot and stomps on the ember sizzling into the carpet.

"Different," Michael says. "Moved on."

I don't like what he is saying, nor his tone of voice, and I ask, "What in the name of fuckery does 'moved on' mean?"

He looks right at me. He has been calm and casual all this time. But now I am the centre of his attention, and it feels as though I am being scrutinised by something massive and way, way beyond my comprehension. "I'm not sure yet," he says. "Isn't that wonderful?"

I look away and take another swig of beer. I close my eyes. The conversation continues, but I think of Michael's watery eyes and the sense that his gaze could bore straight to the centre of my fractured soul.

Theakston's Old Peculier, deep and dark and heavy, a smooth roasty beer with a hint of chocolate and an unmistakeable vinous aftertaste, a *complex* beer, rich and powerful and as familiar to my tongue as the taste of Ashley's skin, the hint of her breath, the tang of sweat on her neck as we make love. Theakston's Old Peculier, the brown bottle still wet and cold even though we had been sitting in Paul's back garden for over an hour, watching him cook and listening to his band's new demo, and Ashley was beside me, drinking her own drink and making me the centre of her universe by never looking at me. That's how I marked the depth of our love: we could be together so completely without touching or saying anything. We breathed the same air.

Paul cooked steak and chicken quarters and pork loin chops on the gas barbeque. I could feel the heat of it from where I sat, but even on that hot summer day it was not uncomfortable. He sprinkled spiced oil over the steak and stood back when a gush of flame licked upward for a few seconds, sealing the meat. The pork was thickly coated in a peanut glaze, slowly bubbling and turning dark.

"You honestly think they'll close it?" Ashley said. We had been talking about the recent outbreak of bird flu in France, and the Prime Minister's comments about closing the channel tunnel. There had been a lot of piss-taking in the media about that: a threat from the skies, so the PM proposes protecting his nation by closing a tunnel beneath the sea. But as ever, Paul had theories about it that seemed to hold water. He spent a lot of time on the 'net, mixing with other conspiracy-theory fanatics and picking up information from sources I wouldn't even know how to find. Most people thought he was plain nuts. I'd known him long enough to know that was not entirely true.

More often than not, Paul was right. Ashley had only known him for as long as she'd known me, almost a year. I believed she was beginning to see what Paul was all about.

"I'm sure they will," he said, turning a steak. "It's just a matter of time. The flu's already jumped from bird to human in fifteen cases. Now if it starts getting passed from person to person, we'll have to take advantage of our island state. And an island doesn't have a direct link to the mainland. The tunnel's always been a bad idea.

I know a guy who worked on it, old bloke down the pub, and he and I have had lots of chats about it. It's common knowledge they left the tunnelling machines buried in the walls down there, and most people believe it's because it would have been too expensive to bring them back out."

"And that isn't the reason?" Ashley asked.

Paul shook his head. "'Course not. The real reason is, those machines carry nukes. One code, one button, one finger, and the tunnel is closed forever."

Ashley glanced at me and raised an eyebrow, but I just shrugged.

"You don't believe me?" Paul said.

"It's not that," Ashley said, "it's just that… it seems so unlikely."

"Why?" A pork joint was spitting fat and flaming, but Paul's attention was distracted. He hated it when people doubted him. I was one of the few who could see past his fanaticism to the inherent truth in many of his beliefs, and very often that scared me.

"Well, who'd do something like that?"

"The government. The military. Whoever owns them."

"All three?"

"Believe me, sweet cakes, they're all one." Paul went back to cooking, and Ashley moved closer to me so that she could put her hand on my knee.

It turned into one of those afternoons and evenings that you remember forever. At the time it's just another drink, another meal, another long chat with good friends, and you don't perceive the special sheen to the day until much, much later. Then you look back on it and realise that it was one of the days of your life. How could you have not realised what was happening? How can the look in your lover's eye have escaped you, or the sense of peaceful kinship between you and the guy who'd been your friend since you were nine, and who would die thirty years later, just two days before the woman you had loved all that time? But that's the thing about these most special of days: you can't *make* them special. You can't sit there and think to yourself, Right, this is going to be a day I remember forever. They just imprint themselves on your brain: the way your girl looks at you, something your friends says, the taste of a steak, the sensation of getting pleasantly drunk while the world goes on about you. You may forget that day for ten years, but then you'll be grocery shopping, agonising over what to have for dinner, and a particular moment from that day will leap into your head, a snapshot accompanied by an intense emotional recollection. It's as powerful as déjà vu, and you'll say to yourself, Damn, that was a fucking good time! I wish it could all be like that again.

But wishing cannot make it so. And you may think that times are worse than they once were, but you know what? Another ten years on, you'll have a flashback to that shopping trip and the evening that followed it when you ate a good curry and drank Wolf Blass and watched the God-awful remake of *The Haunting*, and that too will become one of the days of your life.

Sometimes days age like a good wine, and only time can make them special.

THREE

DOUBLE DROP

We offer Michael the bed-settee in the old games room. It's back past the kitchen, tucked in between the utility room and a store room stacked with old, bad family portraits. Michael is grateful, and as he stands to wish us goodnight I think he sheds a tear. "Goodnight," he says, and I nod. The Theakston's has made a blur of my senses. I like that.

He leaves the room, and we all fall quiet as we hear his footsteps retreat along the hallway. *He must feel very uncomfortable*, I think. *Waiting to hear us start talking about him.* But something strange happens: none of us begins. The room remains silent but for the spit and crackle of logs settling in the fire.

I rise at the same time as Cordell. "I'm hitting the sack," I say. I smile at the others and leave the room. I think back to that long-ago time with Ashley in Paul's back garden, and remember the day twelve months ago when an explosion ripped the channel tunnel apart, killing thousands and making Britain an island once again. It had not worked, of course. Paul had called me that very evening to say he'd found a sore on his chest.

I walk upstairs, listening to the resounding silence of the people I have come to think of, very quickly, as the last friends I will ever have. And I wonder whether I will live long enough for this to become one of the days of my life.

I meet Jessica on the landing. I am the only one who still tries to talk to her about her past, and sometimes she smiles, offering a phrase or two that paints a bare outline of what she might have been through. I know she's a long way from home. She cycled here, she says she left no one behind. And usually she seems strong.

On the landing, just before she really acknowledges my presence, I see a flash of something in her eyes that I can't quite make out. Perhaps it's madness, or maybe it's fear; both terrify me.

"What do you think?" I ask.

"I think I'm tired."

"But Michael?"

Jessica shrugs. She does that a lot, and I've come to see it as something of a shield, a silent answer that gives nothing away.

"He says things are moving on," I say. And there's that flash in Jessica's eyes again as she turns around and goes to her room.

When I close my door and lean against it, I listen for

crying. But all I hear is silence.

"Wake up."

There's a hand on my forehead. It's cool and comforting, and for a while I am not in the awful here and now. I'm not sure where I am exactly, but it feels safe. It feels *different*. There's no smell or sight to recognise, but I'm in a place where loved ones don't die of a virulent virus out of Africa, and where there's always another bottle of beer in the cupboard, the shop, the brewery. I think of Paul's comment after he rang to tell me he'd found a sore. *The irony of it really grabs my shit. Africa: the cradle of civilisation, and the coffin of its demise. If I thought the world would be here long enough, maybe I'd write a book.*

"Africa," I whisper, and the hand lifts from my forehead.

"Not that far," the voice says, and it is not Paul. "Cornwall will do." I open my eyes.

There's a shape sitting on my bed. Over the past few months I've had several visits from Jacqueline in the middle of the night. There has never been any tension between us, no threats of things getting out of hand, because we both know some of each other's story. The most we did was to lie down side by side and take comfort in each other's presence. But this is not Jacqueline, and I suppose I know that Michael is here even before I open my eyes.

Only Ashley has ever been able to comfort me with a touch.

"Cornwall?" I ask.

"A special place. It's *solid*. Roots planted deep. Up here is too… changeable." He stands and the bed springs creak. At least I know he's real. "Can we have a chat?" he says.

"Of course." I sit up and groan. My legs are aching from all the running up and down the tower yesterday, and I think of the frisson of fear I'd felt when I first saw the motorbike emerging from the dead city. I realise that Michael has yet to tell us any real details about himself or where he has been—the previous evening revealed little—but before I can ask he has flicked a lighter and lit the oil lamp. He brings the chair from beside the door and swings it around, sitting on it backwards. His pose is casual and controlled. There's something about him that disturbs me slightly, but I can't quite place it. Perhaps it's simply that we're here on our own. Yesterday, there was always someone else.

"I'm only here for a short time," Michael says.

"You're not staying?"

He shakes his head. "I have to move on. You're not the only ones left, and I have lots to do."

"There really are others? Like us?"

"Of course. Did you ever think there weren't?"

"But you said they were different, somehow."

"Some of them are, yes. *Most*. But not all."

I look away from him, needing to think. *Did I ever believe that we really were the last ones? A foolish supposition, and yet there have been no signs of anyone else. Nothing at all.*

"You have to go to Cornwall," Michael says. "A place on the north coast. It's called Bar None. It will soon be the last bar on Earth. I think it's somewhere you can be happy with your memories of Ashley."

I stare at him, all movements frozen. Even my heart misses a beat, then races, knocking the breath from me.

"Jacqueline told me her name," he says, but I don't believe him.

"Why Cornwall?"

"I told you, it's a solid place. Bar None will be safe. It's been arranged, and it won't change when the time comes."

"What if I don't want to leave?"

Michael leans forward. "Life is opportunity, and living is the greatest opportunity of all."

"Who are you?"

He smiles, looks at his watch. "Yesterday, I was Michael. But it's gone midnight now, and soon it'll be time for me to go."

"We can't just up and leave," I say. "There could be anything out there."

His face becomes stern. "There is," he says. "Factions that don't agree. People who have moved on. And not everyone who survived is quite as willing to accept things as you and your friends. But survival is an ongoing condition, and the weak must not prevail."

"Are we weak?" I ask. I think of the long days and weeks we've spent here, drinking and theorising and hoping that Jessica's new plants will take, to feed us through the next autumn and winter.

"I think you know the answer to that," he says.

"I want to stay. It's not so bad here."

Michael shakes his head, and I see a brief flash of yellow in his eyes. He sighs, the first sign of impatience, and holds out his hands. "What is there to stay for? Life won't get any easier, believe me. The beer is running out, and at Bar None the cellar is endless. Survive. Evolve."

"Sounds like a fairy tale," I say, smiling.

Michael does not return my smile. "If you like."

I nod, sit up straighter. "What about the others?"

"I've talked to them."

"Already?" I glance at my watch, letting the moonlight illuminate the dials. It's just past one a.m.

"I'm still Michael. To you, and all of them."

"You're not normal." Like a frightened child I gather my duvet, but stop short of pulling it up to my chin.

Michael simply shakes his head, but I'm not sure whether he's denying my accusation, or agreeing.

"I think I'd like you to leave my room." I feel no danger in this man, but there is something else... something different. He's not like me at all.

Michael leans forward, tipping the chair onto its two back legs. They creak beneath his weight. "Things are going to change," he says. "The world has paused, and after it catches its breath it will endeavour to move on. This is your chance to continue with your mantle of survivor."

"Move on?" I ask.

"Wouldn't you?"

I try to think of Ashley, but I see only her tears. "No," I say. "I want to go back."

Michael reaches out and touches my forehead again. It's a strange gesture, unexpected, but it does not feel at all peculiar or threatening. "That's why your memories are so precious," he says. He stands, moves the chair back to the wall and opens the door.

I expect him to pause for one more comment, but he merely glances at me before leaving the room. The door clicks shut quietly, and I hear his soft footfalls along the landing. For an instant they seem to be coming from several directions, as though he walked both left and right upon leaving my room. But then I hear him descending the staircase, and then the front door is unbolted, opened and closed.

I rise and go to my window in time to see Michael mount his motorbike and kick it to life. He cruises along the gravel driveway and passes between the open gates, turning left, uphill and away from the blankness of the dead city.

I look down and see my shadow thrown out over the gravel by my blazing bedroom light, and to the left and right of me are similar shadows, shifting as they are noticed and notice others, retreating, closing blinds and curtains against whatever the night has carried away into its ever-deepening darkness.

I cannot sleep for the rest of that night. I stare at the ceiling, trying to remember the network of cracks but forgetting them each time I close my eyes. I try to think of Ashley—her laugh, smile, touch—but again, it's only the bad times at the end that I can recall. My memory never has been very good. Armageddon seems to have made it worse.

I finally rise at five a.m. and go downstairs. For a few

heartbeats, walking down the massive curved staircase that winds its way to the hallway, I have no idea what I will find. The possibilities suddenly seem endless: Michael has been and gone, and he could have left anything behind. He chose to come and talk to me in the night, but perhaps he had raped Jessica, throttled Cordell, set fire to Jacqueline as she tried to scream above a whisper. None of us knew him, none of us had any idea where he had come from or where he was heading. We ate and drank together all evening, but he succeeded in telling us almost nothing of himself. Our curiosity was piqued, for sure, but somehow the food and drink, and the heat of the fire, calmed us into a sense of peace. We did not ask him about those ambiguous shapes flying above and dipping down to the dead city. We did not ask what he had seen in there. None of us truly challenged him.

My footfall is soft on the hallway's oaken floor. I hear sounds of movement from the kitchen, and a light dances out from that door, a flame disturbed by a soft breeze. There is movement in the Manor's air however still we are, as though voices never stop whispering back and forth.

"Who's there?" someone says.

I walk through the door. "Only me. I couldn't sleep." It's Jessica, dressed in heavy sweatshirt and trousers, arms wrapped around her chest as she waits for the kettle to boil. We've got through three gas canisters since we've been here. Two left.

"Nor me," she says. "Tea?"

I nod. *Should I mention Michael?* I glance toward the rear of the kitchen, through the open door where he had gone to sleep the previous night. Jessica is making no attempt to be quiet. She must know he's no longer there.

"I usually sleep really well," she says. "Keeping my days busy. Keeps my mind busy too." She adds more tea to the pot and fetches another mug from the cupboard. It's powdered milk, of course, but we've all become used to it. "I'm exhausted by the time we all crash out. And the beer helps."

"It seems to help us all," I say. It's something we don't talk about very much, our growing dependency on alcohol to see us through. None of us has what would have been called "a problem" in times just gone—our stocks don't allow for that—but we all look forward to that communal couple of drinks each evening. We don't want to spoil the effect by talking about it.

I think it stitches us to the past. And for a while, perhaps it helps us forget the future.

"Last night, though…" The kettle boils and she pours, but I can see that she's distracted.

"Shall I start breakfast?" I say. "Fried potatoes?"

"He says we have to move on," she says. She stirs the tea slowly, methodically. "Cornwall."

"Bar None," I say.

Jessica glances up. "I was wondering."

"And the others?"

"Easier if he did visit them as well. But we'll see. Yes, fried potatoes sound good."

"Don't they always?" I take the cup of tea from her hands and set it down beside the wide gas stove.

Preparing and cooking food usually frustrates me, but

today I find the process calming. The potatoes are old, so I have to cut out the eyes, and then peeling them takes several minutes. I slice them into half-inch sections, dropping them into a bowl of water to wash out some of the starch. Then I lay them out on a cloth, salt them, fire up a burner and coat a frying pan with a layer of oil. I drop in some garlic salt and a pinch of dried herbs, and as the oil starts to bubble I place the potato slices side by side. Jessica sits silently behind me, though I can feel her eyes on the back of my head. We're comfortable together, friends.

We sit and eat, the truth hanging between us seeming to enliven the air, and as we finish the others come down. Jacqueline mentions that she could not sleep, and Cordell goes straight to the stove, firing up the burner and cooking more potatoes. He does not speak, but I know he has something to say.

When everyone is there, making tea or eating or just sitting at the table, I stand and say, "Bar None."

Nobody seems very surprised.

"And now he's gone," the Irishman says. "He can't explain himself, and he never even told us where he comes from."

"There are five of us here," Jessica says. Her long hair looks wild after a night of not sleeping, like an unkempt halo. "I saw him ride away around two this morning. How could he have come to all of us?"

"How long was he with you?" Jacqueline says.

Jessica shrugs. "Half an hour."

"Me too," Cordell says.

Silence, but for the sizzle of frying potatoes.

"Well, who's to say anything he said is true?" Cordell says.

"I believe him." I walk to the sink and swill my cup from the bucket of water standing there. *Do we really have to leave all this?* I think. *The garden, the tower, the spring? Where will be get our water from on the road? Will the mains still be working in some places? Is it safe to drink it from a reservoir? What about the other survivors Michael mentioned, the good ones and the bad? And the other things he hinted at... those "factions."* The thoughts rampage through my mind, setting me on edge and causing me to shiver. I look out the window and up the slope toward the tower. There are several rabbits dotted around its base, taking in the sun.

"What's there to believe?" Cordell says. Jacqueline is whispering something as well, but voices raise and none of us can hear what she's saying.

I stare from the window for a while, not joining in the exchange. It soon becomes so that I can't tell who is saying what, who wants to go, who wants to stay. Through all of it I hear Jacqueline's whisper, a background to the argument that will always be there when it's over. I know that we will hear her soon, and I know what she will say, because I'm thinking it as well.

"Quiet," I say. The word breaks through at just the right moment, and the kitchen falls almost silent.

"We're running out of everything," Jacqueline says, her voice low but, for the first time, strong. "The spring is still there, but maybe it'll dry up in the summer. Jessica is planting the garden, and I hope it will grow, but if the spring dries up...? The food and beer is almost gone.

We'll have to go out there to get some more, but Michael told me everything has gone bad. Even the tinned stuff, and the food in cans. *All bad*, he said."

"We're running out of everything," Cordell says, seemingly tasting the words. He looks up at me and I cannot read his expression.

"Except hope," I say. "I still have hope."

"Do you really?" I'm not sure who says it, but it does not matter.

"Yes. And can any of us say that Michael was just another survivor?"

Cordell is frowning, turning his head this way and that, and finally he holds up his hand and says, "Quiet."

We fall silent. Cordell says nothing. Instead, he walks to the door leading into Jessica's hopeful garden, draws the bolts, turns the heavy key, opens the door and goes outside.

We all follow, and then I hear what caught his attention. The distant, even rattle of an idling motorbike.

Cordell sets off at a run. I follow, and I hear footsteps behind me as well. I hope all of us are running; it seems important to me that all five see what is to be seen. For a while the crunch of feet on gravel drowns out the motor as we race along the driveway toward the wide gates.

The sun is rising almost directly above the gates. It warms my face, spilling through the trees, catching the million hints of sprouting leaves. The plagues may have come and gone, but the world is still alive, continuing as it always has except without the interference of humankind.

Things are going to change, Michael said.

None of us says anything as Cordell passes between the gates. I follow, sparing a glance for the huge wrought iron constructs, wondering where they were made and who worked on them, and how many days someone invested in forming, twisting and welding the metal together. So much creation and love, and now they would stand here until time dragged them from their mounts and covered them with dust.

"Oh, shit," Cordell says. I come to a standstill beside him, our arms touching, and stare at the motionless motorbike.

It rests on its stand a hundred feet up the lane. It has been left at the side of the road, its motor ticking over, wheel turned to prevent it from rolling backward down the slight incline. The hedge beside it is evergreen, tall and full, and Michael knew that none of us would be able to see it from the Manor.

"It's just like he said he found it," I say.

Cordell walks to the bike and looks around: the ditch, the hedge, across the lane at the lower hedge on that side. "We have to look for him," he says. "He may have fallen off."

"And left the bike on its stand?" the Irishman says, lighting a cigarette.

The others are here now, forming a line across the road as though unwilling to move closer. I walk up beside Cordell and help him look, knowing all the while that we'll find nothing. "Help us, then!" I say. The others spread out, climb a gate into the field, walk along the road's scruffy verge, head back downhill in case he has crawled that way, injured or dying.

We search for half an hour. For some reason no one wants to switch off the motor. As the sun clears the trees to the east I turn the key, and the silence is shattering. "He's gone," I say.

"Why did he leave the bike?" Jessica asks. No one answers, because no one knows.

"Let's get it back to the Manor," Cordell says. "It might come in useful."

"When we leave?" Jessica says.

I look around at everyone, see the mixture of fear and confusion. "Let's just get back where we can talk," I say. This is the first time in six months we have all been away from the Manor at the same time, and it feels strange. It's as though by coming out here we have abandoned the place, if only for a few minutes. We all need to get back.

Walking through the gates, seeing the Manor and the folly up on the hill touched by the sun, it suddenly looks like nowhere I have ever been.

I go straight down to the cellar to see what we have left. It's a comfort thing. Everyone understands, and the Irishman accompanies me.

"So what *is* your damn name?" I ask him.

He runs his fingers along a shelf of bottles, slipping from label to label, name to name. "All I have left."

I remember sitting in The Hanbury's garden in Caermaen drinking Marston's Double Drop, a golden ale with a fruity malt aroma, a bright and yeasty taste with a bitter, caramel finish, cool going down and calm as it dulled my senses, while all around us families ate basket meals and bickered, kids scraped their knees hiding beneath the heavy timber tables, mothers fussed and spread sun cream and fathers ruffled their sons' hair and smiled as their daughters ran off to find other girls, sit in the shadow of the hedge, play with their dolls and pretend to be mothers themselves.

Ashley and I had been talking about starting a family, and I knew from the look on her face what was to come next.

"Does all this noise bother you?" she asked.

Yes, I thought. *I like drinking in peace.* "'Course not," I said. "Kids having fun. What better noise could there be?"

She stared at me, then the corners of her mouth turned up in that coy Charlize Theron smile. She leaned in close. "You fuckin' wit' my head?"

"Not your head, no."

"Hey, later, we've only just got here."

We sat in silence for a while, the noise breaking around us like a fast-flowing stream parting around stones. *Children.* In many ways I wanted that, but there was something sad and intimidating about leaving behind everything we had; the freedom, the lack of responsibility. We were fighting against the tide of Ashley's body clock and struggling against the persuasive storm of evolution ringing through our blood. Soon, we would go with the flow.

I looked into Ashley's eyes, and she read me like a book.

"It won't be so bad," she said. She looked at the kids causing chaos around the pub garden, stroked the back of her neck with one hand, hair falling across her eyes. I did not see her again for what felt like hours. When she looked back at me her eyes were moist, but I would never know whether they were tears of sadness or joy.

I did not ask. It was always easier not to, and it was starting out to be a nice day. I always was one for the moment, keen to keep things calm and comfortable and quiet, and there were a million things I should have said and done which remained unsaid and undone because of that particular cowardice.

"It'll be fine," I said. I finished my pint and stood to get another. Ashley offered up her glass and I negotiated my way across the garden, looking down instead of forward so that I did not trip over any kids.

I bought another Double Drop, though the wide selection of ales there was tempting. The Hanbury had long been a favourite haunt of mine, and since we met, Ashley had also fallen in love with the place. She drank halves as I quaffed pints, and though I knew that she was not as obsessed with ales as I was, I appreciated the gesture. There was something about love in that. She didn't really like Japanese movies or sushi either, but she indulged for me, and I ate the curry she liked and watched the occasional episode of *ER,* and we both knew that compromise was a big part of falling in love and *staying* in love. So far, we had done very well indeed.

Later that day we moved across the wide river bridge and sat on the opposite bank outside the Veil's Arms. The pub had always intrigued me, and when I finally asked, the landlord told me that the name was something to do with a seventeenth-century highwayman, his love for a local farmer's daughter, and the piece of clothing of hers he wore when he was being hanged. The old oak tree in the pub garden was reputedly the hanging tree, and one of the thick lower branches bore a ring of knotted bark that was allegedly the wound made by the rope. It was a rich, interesting story, and the pub took full advantage of the opportunities afforded by it. You could order a Hangman's Lunch from its varied menu, drink a pint of locally brewed Highwayman's Best Effort, or peruse various etchings and paintings of the events whilst taking a piss. I was glad they had not gone too far; the next step was surely a mannequin hanging from the tree and a photographer charging to have your picture taken holding the rope.

Ashley and I sat on the grassed riverbank and watched the river rise as the tide came in. It was peaceful, warm, and the sound of kids playing drifted across the river from The Hanbury. We talked inconsequentialities because the important stuff had already been said, and I stuck to the Double Drop, and as the sun started to sink toward the wooded western hills I had a comfortable buzz about me.

"How much of the same water do you think flows back up-river when the tide comes in?" Ashley said.

"Er…" I shook my head. The ripples in the muddy water's surface caught the sinking sun, giving the river a clayish texture never seen in the day.

"I mean, all that water flows down from the hills, picking up sediment, carrying leaves and twigs, rolling stones. The odd corpse of a sheep or bird. And it dumps it all into the estuary. Then a few hours later the tide rises, and this part of the river goes up, and some of the water flows back in."

"I'm not quite sure that's *exactly* what happens," I said. It struck me that I had spent many days of my adult life staring at a river with a pint in my hand, but in truth I had no definite idea of how rivers really worked. This type of revelation often hit me, and it worried me that I could go through life understanding so little. I was afraid I would lose my way.

"You see the same things flowing in and out with the tide, sometimes," Ashley said. "Almost as if the river can't decide whether or not to move on."

"Er… do you want another drink?"

"Gin and tonic," she said, never taking her eyes from the water. "Like life. That's confusing too."

"This is getting *way* too fucking deep for me," I said, and as I stood Ashley glanced up at me without smiling. I carried that look with me into the pub, stood with it at the bar and brought it back out, turning it over in my mind and trying to identify exactly what I had seen in her eyes. Impatience? Frustration?

Hatred?

I hurried back with her drink and sat down so that our arms were touching. I was almost afraid to speak.

"Cheers," she said, tapping my glass with her own.

"Bottoms up," I said.

"Later, if you're lucky." She grinned, leaned in close, and everything felt fine.

We agree to leave the next day. Michael had a power

over us, that is evident in the others' faces as we sit around the huge dining room table. There is discussion and dissent, but mostly it is half-hearted. We all know that we will be going, because Michael made it so. He was not here for long. He came one afternoon and left that night, but in the space of twelve hours he forced us to make more real decisions than we had in six months.

Jessica cooks some food and brings it in. I still have oil on my hands from tinkering with the motorbike, but I am suddenly ravenous, and I eat with gusto. Some of us have only recently had breakfast yet our hunger is vast. Strange. I watch everyone else eating and try to see behind their expressions, hear what Michael said to them, feel the weight his gaze had on their eyes as well as my own.

"Who was he?" I say at last. I'm sure the others have been thinking it—the air is thick with the question—but I'm glad that I'm the one to verbalise it at last.

"Just a visitor," Cordell says. "He's travelled, while we've stayed put. He knows more of what's been going on. So he decided to tell us, help us."

"What a load of bollocks," the Irishman says. "'A visitor'? He rode up from the city. What was he doing there? What about those things we sometimes see above the city? See, but never talk about, because they don't fit in with our comfortable little plan of 'stay put and fuck the rest'? And he left his fuckin' bike running outside the gates. What was that all about?"

"That's the same way he found it," Jessica says.

"Yeah, so he says."

"But we've all agreed that we're going," I say. "We all

believe in this Bar None place he told us about?"

We eat in silence for a few seconds, none of us wishing to meet another's eyes.

"No reason not to believe," Jessica says quietly. "And it's something to do."

"Well then, tomorrow," Cordell says. "We go tomorrow. And in the meantime, other than packing a few bags with what little we have, I suggest we take a drink." He stands and walks from the room, aiming for the stairs and the door to the basement below. None of us calls him back. It is not even midday, but society is dead. Who gives a shit?

"Bottoms up," I say. The others smile and nod, and I know that today won't last for very long.

I go to help Cordell bring up the last of the bottles. There are more than we think, and it takes us several trips. Jessica and the Irishman arrange the bottles on the table in the living room, and by the time we make our final trip there is quite an array on offer.

"Forty-two," Jessica says. "What a day."

I pull a bottle opener from my pocket and flip the lid on a bottle of Golden Glory. I raise it and salute everyone else in the room. Then I take a long drink. Peach, melon and malts on the nose, a hoppy, fruity bite, and a long-lasting sweet aftertaste. I smack my lips and sigh. "I love beer," I say. Even on my own, I always honour such a good brew.

The others select their bottles and give their own toasts.

"Good health," Cordell says.

"I name this shit The End," Jessica says.

"Drink is the feast of reason and the flow of soul."

"A mouth of a perfectly happy man is filled with beer."

"Here's to home," the Irishman says. "I'll never see her again." He turns away to take his first drink, and I stare into the neck of my own bottle, thinking of Ashley and knowing that everyone has a similar thought. Except maybe Jessica. She's an enigma, and sometimes I think she's lost nothing at all.

We'll never really be all together, I think. *Not the way we've been introduced. Maybe we're friends, but we'll never know each other. There's far too much to know. Too much lost, too much forgotten, too much we'd like to forget. Fate has made us full of secrets.*

"To Bar None," I say, raising my bottle. The others follow, and again I am struck by our easy belief in a midnight man's story.

We drink throughout that final day at the Manor. Lunchtime comes and goes, the world outside exists without our seeing it or taking part, and we sit mostly in silence and finish the last of the beer. Occasionally someone leaves the room to go and pack their bags, but they are never away for very long. There's not much to pack—clothes, a book, the few personal effects most of us still own—and he or she is always keen to return to the living room. There's something very much like a family about us today.

Cordell falls asleep after several bottles and starts to snore. Jacqueline smiles, hiding the expression behind her hand. She's so delicate and brittle, I can't believe she's survived the end of the world.

"So is this really it?" the Irishman asks, as if hearing my thoughts.

"Well, when I look out there I don't see very much left," Jacqueline says.

"I do." Jessica stands and moves to the window, becoming a part of the view. "I see trees sprouting buds. Daffodils are flowering along the hedge at the front of the garden, and others have sprouted ready to bloom in the flower beds below this window. Snowdrops among the trees over there. Green shoots of bluebells, and we'll see the flowers themselves soon. Birds feeding on insects in the trees, butterflies here and there. The grass is lush and starting to grow again, and I'm glad none of us could be bothered trying to cut it. I've never seen it so green."

"You seem to have forgotten the stinking dead city bulging with two hundred thousand corpses," the Irishman says.

"I didn't forget. That's what's ended. I'm just looking at what's continuing."

"We're continuing," I say.

"This?" Jacqueline says. Her soft voice has turned surprisingly harsh. Drink doesn't agree with her, and I always get on edge when she's starting her fourth or fifth bottle. "This is hardly continuing. We're dead but breathing."

"It's still an existence for me," Jessica says, and her breath mists the glass in the window.

"Yeah, but you're weird." Jacqueline lobs her empty bottle and it smashes in the stone fireplace.

"He said everything's going to change," I say.

We drink, and think, and the room is silent for a long time.

That evening, the last of the beer gone, bottles smashed in the fireplace, glass spilling across the carpet like dying embers of a cold fire, I open the patio doors and stand on the gravelled garden area with Cordell, Jessica and the Irishman. Jacqueline has gone to her room, and we can hear the sounds of the Manor settling around us as the heat leaves its stone walls. The sun has gone, leaving a bloody smear across the horizon. Some trees catch the light, and a few clouds echo pink and orange.

"It's a long way," Cordell says. "Could be anything out there."

"Anyone," Jessica says.

We're not watching anything in particular, but I see the way the setting sun continues to hang from the branches of trees, dripping from them, clinging on even after the horizon has grown dark.

Things are going to change, I think. I glance at the others and know that they have seen it too.

FOUR

GOLDEN GLORY

When morning comes we're keen to leave. We pack the two Range Rovers we found in the Manor's garages when we first arrived. Cordell checks them over—tyre pressures, oil levels—although I know he has been tending the vehicles regularly for months. It was something to kill the time, but I also think he always knew there would be a time when we needed them. Most of us, me included, rarely thought beyond a few days ahead.

I have volunteered to ride Michael's motorbike. I am the most experienced, and the thought of riding alone appeals to me. The bike is something of a talisman in my mind, a physical proof of Michael's presence. It was only the night before last that he spoke to me—spoke to us all—but already I'm finding it hard to believe that he was ever here. He has caused us to move on, yet I can barely remember his face or voice. If I close my eyes it's almost there, like someone's name on the tip of your tongue, but there's nothing that quite jars the memory and makes it concrete.

But the bike is solid, the bike is there. Its seat is worn, its tyres old and nearing the ends of their lives, and oil has spattered much of the engine and congealed. I took a rag to it earlier in an attempt to clean it off, but succeeded only in smearing the oil onto new places. It's been a long time since I looked after a bike, and this one is older than any I have ever ridden. It almost belongs in a museum. *It's worth a fortune*, I told Cordell that morning, and I smile yet again at his response. *Gets you where you need to go, it's worth your fuckin' life.* I have kick-started it several times already, and every time I take comfort in its familiar voice.

We're ready to leave by mid-morning. Hangovers have mostly lifted now, and there's an unexpected air of excitement amongst our small group. I had expected the beginnings of our journey to be downbeat and filled with dread, but even Jacqueline is smiling, and Cordell is keeping any doubts to himself. My thoughts lie at journey's end, and I guess everyone else is thinking the same way. I'm trying to imagine Bar None, the last bar in the world, sitting aloof on a Cornish cliff overlooking the wild sea, seagulls buzzing its old slate roof, windows long-ago painted shut against bitter ocean winds, walls painted white and chimney smoking a welcome. Inside… I cannot see. Michael has given me nothing for that.

I dwell little on the trip between now and then. The hundred and fifty miles of open countryside, dead towns and cities, burnt out power stations, abandoned cars, impassable roads, fields spotted with the humps of rotten cattle, rivers swollen with spring rains and bodies from the hills, and other things we cannot prepare for, or even imagine. We are not the only survivors, we know that since Michael came. I try not to think about meeting others. When I do, the outcome I envisage is never good.

I glance down at the city, pleased to see that the skies above it are empty today. Those things have never bothered us. But they are there. Their impossible truth is something we have never had the confidence to really discuss.

"So are we ready?" Cordell says. He's at the Manor's front door, looking out at us where we all stand on the gravel driveway. The door is open behind him, and looking inside feels like staring into the past. I can see the staircase that I will never climb again, ever. The banister already seems to have gathered a veneer of dust, and I'm sure I can make out a huge spider's web on the upstairs landing.

"I am," Jessica says. "Never thought I'd have wanderlust, but I just want to get out of here now."

"Yeah," the Irishman says, "this doesn't feel like our fuckin' pad anymore."

He's right. I look at the Manor's upstairs windows and they're impenetrable.

Jacqueline sighs, nods, then climbs into the first Range Rover and starts it up. The growl of the engine startles a flock of birds from a tree in the garden, and they loop around our heads a couple of times before disappearing over the building's roof. I imagine them following the contours of the land until they reach the tower, roost in the Manor builder's folly, ready to watch us leave and reclaim their home again.

"We should leave the doors open," I say. I expect one or two of the others to disagree, but only the Irishman offers a reply.

"He's right. We won't be back."

Cordell nods and walks to the second Range Rover. "Don't get too far ahead," he says to me quietly as he passes by. He's frowning. For the very first time that day, I feel a sense of fear at what we are about to do.

I mount the bike and kick it to life. We have already agreed to a preliminary route, and I tick off the road names and numbers in my mind. It sounds easy enough, but it's inevitable that we will encounter obstructions on our way. There will be abandoned vehicles of all kinds, untamed undergrowth, and perhaps fallen trees from the winter storms just gone by.

And maybe other things, Cordell said.

Like what? Jacqueline asked.

People.

I zip my jacket and make sure the woollen gloves allow me adequate sensation. I have no helmet—Michael came without one—and my glasses will have to suffice in place of goggles. *People*, Cordell said. I think of that now, and every bad apocalyptic movie I have ever seen comes back to me again. Roadblocks manned by cannibals, a river of zombies stumbling along the tarmac, biker gangs raping women and slitting men's throats, road gangs shooting a driver for the gallon of gas in his or her tank… Each situation seems ridiculous individually, but I know that

Cordell is right. There *will* be people out there, and many of them may not have weathered the past six months as well as we have.

What do we do if someone asks where we're going? Jessica asked.

Tell them to mind their fucking business, the Irishman said.

We have an air rifle and a shotgun. It's not a country where automatic weapons and rocket launchers are lying around to be claimed, yet there are places where a determined gang could find such things.

I shake my head and rev the bike. Jacqueline smiles shyly behind the windscreen of the first Range Rover, the Irishman sitting beside her. Cordell starts the second vehicle, adding to the noise. Jessica is his companion.

I'm on my own. And this is no time to get scared.

I lead the way along the gravel driveway. I move slowly to begin with, slipping into second gear and leaving it there for a while. The bike rides smoothly, crunching over gravel and responding well. It feels good beneath me. I'm warm and safe, my thinning hair combed by the breeze.

I can hear the large Range Rovers following me, their heavy wheels crushing gravel aside whereas mine simply rides over the surface. They contain our worldly goods, everything the five of us owns: our food, a few bottles of wine, two guns, gallons of water stored in old milk churns, and a selection of books from the Manor's library. We are carrying some of our past and all of our present with us, and for a while the future will exist only until the next bend in the road.

I reach the gates, pass between them and turn right without pause. As I straighten and shift gears I look to my right, through the budding hedge at the Manor. It looks so old and badly maintained, so lifeless, and I wonder whether it has borne that appearance for the past six months. I thought we brought life to the place, but perhaps not. Even with candles burning in its windows, I think maybe it simply looked haunted. I glance higher at the tower, and for a second I see my own pale face watching from its balcony. I swerve the bike across the road and regain control, then look again. The face has gone. It was never there at all, of course, but its absence makes me eager to be away.

I look over my shoulder, nod at Jacqueline at the wheel of the vehicle behind me, and start to pick up some speed.

That wasn't me, I think. *That wasn't anyone.* I wonder if Michael had sensed me watching him zigzag between stalled vehicles down in the city. I feel no probing eyes on me now, but that is no comfort.

The road bears left and down, passing between a high ceiling of trees whose branches meet overhead. The budding leaves already form something of a canopy, and the road is speckled with their shadows. As spring advances so their shadows will grow until it is sunlight that spots the road. The ebb and flow of nature, the rise and fall of seasons, had always been a fascination for Ashley.

I dreamed of her last night—of course I did, the hops insisted upon it—and her presence in my mind is a comfort, even though I cannot see her.

I know she will be helping me on my way.

And as I think of her strained face again, for the first time ever I am glad that we never had a child.

Golden Glory, one of Badger's finest, pale and gold, crisp and refreshing and sweet, a barbeque beer that binds together outside eating, afternoon drinking and the sound of aircraft Dopplering across the hazy blueness of a late August afternoon, making it a whole, sensory experience that will be remembered as a day of your life. There's something almost sentient about a beer that manages to do that, as though supping Golden Glory is drinking in the flavour of life and the language of God. Three bottles, four, and even with spiced burgers and marinated lamb steaks resting in my stomach, still the ale slipped down well on that endless summer afternoon.

The barbeque was cooling in a far corner of the garden, because we needed no more heat. I was comfortable in a pair of shorts and nothing else, and Ashley was wearing a short summer skirt and a roomy blouse, no bra, her hair tied loosely, sun cream speckling the fine hairs on her neck and smeared across her ears where I had failed to rub it in properly. Too much effort. I could just about lift the glass from lap to mouth and back again, and I knew that later we would go inside, shower and make love. Skin warmed by the sun, we would make sure we moisturised each other, and then lie atop the bed and draw the curtains, sweating and cooling again in our bedroom's shadows.

A robin sat on our garden fence, chirping at us. It was almost tame. A wisp of cloud had appeared high up, barely moving as though uncertain of which way to go. I was trying to make out images in the cloud, but it and my mind were too vague to form a solid shape. For no reason I could properly discern, that troubled me.

Sometimes it's a day of your life for all the wrong reasons.

Ashley rose from her chair, groaning like an old woman, and stretched. Her blouse rose up and offered me a peek at several inches of taut belly. She rubbed at her hair, stretched back to look up at the sky, and I could make out the shape of her nipples beneath the material. I hummed appreciatively.

"Thought you were asleep," she said.

"You just woke me up."

"Another drink?" She grabbed the glass from my lap and walked toward the house.

"Just one more," I said. "Then I think I need some aftersun."

"Me too," she said without turning around.

"I have a handy applicator."

She glanced back, smiled, and as she passed through the back door she flipped up the back of her skirt, flashing her buttocks. I followed her into the kitchen, watched her carefully pouring another two bottles of Golden Glory, and we never finished those bottles. It was an absolutely perfect day, hued with an unspoken certainty that thrilled us both.

Next day Ashley's period came, three weeks late, and perfection took its leave.

I follow the lane left and right down the hillside, aiming

for the river that borders one side of the dead town, and already this feels like an alien place. The new growth in the hedgerows had been unchecked this spring, allowed to spread untouched by shears or tractor or the wing-mirrors of cars. It bulges out into the road, fresh thin shoots branching off older brown limbs, and buds spot them green. It's not preventing our travel, but I have to drive down the centre of the road to avoid being whipped around the face. I hear the vehicles behind me scraping past here and there, wood bearing on metal like troubled chatter. The road itself is littered with winter's fallen leaves. With no traffic to clear them away the leaves have remained, forming a damp, muddied layer across the tarmac. It's not too slippery right now, because we haven't had rain for almost two weeks, but I still ride carefully.

The motorbike feels comfortable beneath me. It's responsive and obedient, taking me across flat, level surfaces, dodging around small humps in the road that may be buried branches or other things hidden by fallen leaves. My arms start to ache soon after leaving the Manor, but it's not an unpleasant sensation. I can feel the power of the machine transmitted up through my bones, and it feels good.

I reach the end of the narrow lane and let the bike coast to a standstill. The Range Rovers stop behind me, and I hear doors opening, feet crunching on the road. Nobody speaks, because there is so much to say.

The lane emerges out onto the dual carriageway that follows the course of the river past the town. There are a few buildings on this side of the waterway—a petrol station, a fast food restaurant hunkered low in a lay-by, a terrace of old houses still looking angry at the road's intrusion on their long front gardens—but the real town starts directly across the carriageway and over the river. We're still slightly elevated here, because I stopped a hundred meters from the side of the main road. I sense a definite boundary: behind us is the Manor and the time we spent there; before us, once we are on the road, lies a future hinted at by a man who came and went in one day. We can see into the first streets of the city, and this is a very private moment for us all.

I have not been this close to a town for six months. I have watched from the relative safety of the folly, seen winter and spring settle across this dead place, but I have not really been close enough to *see*. One of the blocks of trendy riverside apartments across from us has been gutted by fire, its steel-framed roof warped and angry. The rendered façade is scorched black, windows smashed, and in the small garden leading down to the water lay several shapes that could be burnt furniture or dead people. The sun is at just the right angle to shine through the shattered windows, and even from this distance I can see the shapes of picture frames hanging askew on walls, and the shadow of a fallen ceiling. From the folly I had noted this place as a smear of black on the otherwise blinding white façade of the riverfront properties. Here, the detail is depressing.

A body is hanging from a third-storey balcony several properties along from the burnt building. It's neck has been stretched to an impossible length, and I'm amazed it's still hanging there at all. The glint of bone shows through tattered clothing. The head is a mass of dirty blonde hair, and I can just make out one silver shoe, sharp against the corpse's uncertain outline.

There are abandoned cars on the dual carriageway, most of them parked along the hard shoulder, windows gritty and dusted from the winter downpours. The rain still bears dust, and Cordell thinks that there may have been a war somewhere far away in those long, final days. Even as death stalked the drivers they obeyed old habits. The cars are mostly well parked, only a few edging noses or rears out into the inside lane. But there are also those that are not parked at all, and it's these that makes me think we will never get more than a few miles.

To the south, a crash has left a shiny black scar across both lanes of the southbound carriageway. The dark remains of several cars and a truck are twisted together, and the fire that consumed them six months before also melted and reset the road. I can see an easy way past along the hard shoulder, but there will be more accidents like this.

I keep glancing up at the sky. None of those flying things makes itself known, and for that I am glad. This close, we would be able to see exactly what they are.

"Nothing in the sky," Cordell says. The others are looking as well. Yes, we're all glad.

We stand there for some time, all of us looking at this place we have only seen from a distance since the plagues. The detail is shocking, humbling, and it hits me all over again that things will never be the same. *Things are going to change*, Michael said.

The smell here is not too bad. I feel the breeze kissing

the nape of my neck, a sign that the prevailing wind is carrying the city away from us. But still a hint of its decay hangs in the air, old rot and new devastation. I try to imagine all those thousands of places abandoned or filled with dead, and the overall image is as it always has been: a place of disease, stink, decay, scavenging animals and perhaps scavenging survivors as well. A place where none of us has any desire at all to go. There are homes in there with the family sitting dead around a laden dining table, one last meal interrupted by death. There are gardens filled with the remains of last year's unpicked fruit and vegetables, greenhouses still sealed and rank with rotten tomatoes, cucumbers, marrows and seedlings. There are bodies in gutters with their faces ripped off by wild dogs. Cinemas and theatres are filled with corpses, melting down together as decay does its work, because in the last days they were using such large public places as temporary morgues. The parks are also filled with the dead, some buried, many laid in piles alongside holes that will never be filled. Excavators sit like silent monsters beside them, perhaps with their drivers still at the controls. Much of the dying happened slowly but right at the end, when panic gave way to utter chaos and a regression to a more animal state, the final annihilation was mercifully fast.

And yet we survived. It's something none of us has been able to explain. I have not thought about it for a while, because I still believe myself to be relatively sane. Perhaps not compared to the older gauge of sanity—I dream, I scream, and I place value on my life in relation to the ales I have drunk and the memories those tastes inspire—but it works for me. We all have our ways to get by.

"It's the future that's important," Jessica says. "Not what we see now, all this *old* stuff."

"I sat over there once," Jacqueline says quietly. She points over the road and across the river at the expensive waterside apartments. I'm not sure whether she's indicating the spread of fire-gutted buildings, but I don't think it matters. "Sat on a balcony while Roger made gin martini cocktails. We watched boys swimming in the river, and later some adults went down there and stripped to swim. I was amazed at how unabashed they were. Naked, in front of everyone else. Roger smiled at me and touched the back of my neck." She touches herself there hesitantly, as though afraid that her fingers will feel someone else.

"We don't need to go across there," Cordell says. "The bridge is clear apart from a bike, but we don't need to go across there. We go around. Everywhere like this, we go around, until we reach Cornwall."

I glance at the road bridge and make out the shape of an abandoned bicycle straddling the white line at its highest point. I wonder where its rider had gone all those months ago. We can't see the actual surface of the river from here.

"I agree," I say. "There's nothing for us there."

"That's history," the Irishman says. And I shiver, because for an instant I'm certain he is right. If we try to cross the bridge and enter the dead town, we will find ourselves somewhere else entirely. Because right now we're looking at the past, and soon, as spring progresses and summer looms, nature will begin to look forward.

Lawns will go wild, plant pots will seed themselves farther away, gardens will become unkempt and start probing limbs and roots beneath patios, toward walls and through the gaps of open windows.

"I remember it differently," I say.

"Let's go." Jacqueline climbs into her Range Rover and starts the engine. The noise brings us all around, and as I mount the motorbike and kick it to life the town seems to fade from my vision, covered with a haze from the river perhaps, or drawing away.

I see several large birds perched atop the blackened roof members across the river, and from this far away I cannot recognise the species. *Too small*, I think, but perception is a dangerous thing.

To begin with, it seems that most people wanted to park their cars properly before they died. Perhaps that sudden final onset of the diseases gave them enough time for a few last moments of lucidity. Going to collapse… get off the road… last thing I need is a shunt now… paperwork, insurance claims, all that time that hassle that expense… pull over, pull off… everyone else doing it too… strange…

Cars sit staggered along the hard shoulder, many of them with noses buried in the rears of those in front of them. Trailers lie on their sides or crushed open from impacts, and suitcases, bags, loose clothing and other personal items are strewn across the road. Most of the clothing is a uniform grey, sun, rain, frost and snow having bleached the material and sucked the colour down into the ground.

Other cars have been driven or shoved over the edge of the road and down into the ditch, some of them tipping onto their sides or roofs. Here and there they lie two or even three deep, and there are frequent signs of fires having broken out and ignited the fuel tanks.

I see bodies. I try to look away but cannot. I am the classic road accident rubber-necker, telling myself that I really don't want to see the results of these crashes but looking nonetheless. I thought I'd had my fill of death and suffering in those terrible final weeks of the plagues, but it seems that there is always that deep-set curiosity that can never be assuaged. Many of the cars hold vague shapes behind their windows, but most of the glass is no longer clear. The outside is dusty, and the inside seems to be touched with something as well. I wonder whether the rot of bodies could spread to glass, planting decay in the form of moist moss, greasy fungus, or a film of slickness locked in by windows shut tight.

Nobody wanted to breathe the air outside. Though it was late summer when the end came, still no one knew for sure how the diseases were carried.

Other bodies lie in the road and on the verge, splayed alongside open car doors. I see the white of bone through tears in rotten clothing. The smaller the shapes, the more distressing they are.

Here and there a vehicle has struck the central reservation and ricocheted away, hitting other cars and causing a tangle of wreckage that still sits where it happened. None of them were travelling very fast—the road was packed with people escaping the cities—but damage was exacerbated when vehicles following on behind shoved the shunted cars to the side of the road. They left the occupants trapped inside as they passed by.

They would have, I think. *Can't open those windows, not when there may be germs outside, or infected people inside, disease-carrying flies...*

I can barely imagine how bad it must have been. I suppose my own journey had been performed in relative comfort, three days after the end came. Ashley had started to smell badly by then, and I couldn't find the strength of body or mind to bury her. That was way too final. Ashley, my love, could never be below the ground. So I had left, and gone cross-country, and at the end of that first day travelling I had seen Cordell standing at the gates of the Manor.

I ride the bike slowly along the road, and already I'm trying to calculate how long this trip will take. On a normal day it would be a three hour journey at least, not allowing for any toilet stops or coffee breaks, hold-ups on the Severn Bridge or traffic queues on the perpetually road-worked M5. Now, travelling at thirty instead of eighty miles per hour, it is a day's journey.

But I know that there would be much more than this to hold us up.

FIVE

OLD EMPIRE

When I drink Marston's Old Empire ale—malty, sweet, a gentle bitter finish—I can remember the first time I recognised nature for what it really was. I remember because it was a weekend I spent in a cottage in the Welsh mountains with the two best friends of my teens, Clive and Rob, drinking Old Empire and accepting whatever strange effects so many bottles of that potent brew presented. None of us had ever bothered with drugs, and even at that young age we were true acolytes of brewed hops. Rob had gone through a lager-drinking stage when he was seventeen, suffering much haranguing from me and Clive. But two years later he recognised it for what it really was—the gassy emission from Satan's dick—and he was back with us on the beer.

Ahh, the Heavens we found in so many pint glasses, in so many pubs. By the time I was thirty it was almost a way of life, but even at nineteen beer had a huge effect on me. Perhaps there's something in it, a chemical we're not quite sure of that reacts with the human mind, building a precious bridge between amber fluid and the psychic solidity of our thoughts. What I've always loved about drinking beer is that there's no real snob value attached to it. Go to a local beer festival and you'll pay the same amount for a new local brew as for that year's Best Beer winning brew. A half-pint glass, a tug on the handle, and a taste explosion that moves you one step closer to God.

I like wine, but I despise the culture of snobbery and pomposity built around it. A decent five-pound bottle honestly tastes better to me than the three-hundred-pound bottles I've tried, and I have tried them. Talked into it by friends, offered a glass of something special by work colleagues and some of Ashley's family, and while they haw and har and delight in the sheer decadence of a glass of wine worth more than an OAP's weekly cheque, I reach for the Jacob's Creek and have a much finer time.

So that weekend in Wales, when nature hit me between the eyes for the first time, was informed by the strong taste of one of Marston's finest, allegedly brewed to be shipped to India, though it never made it there. Whether that was simply publicity or fact, I was glad. It was a superb ale, and for the rest of my life I associated its taste with my true coming-of-age.

On the second day in the cottage, I volunteered to walk to the local farm to buy some eggs. We'd brought sausages, bacon and mushrooms, but a fry-up is naked without fried eggs. I took a pocketful of change and a head full of morning-after with me. Not a hangover, as such, more a woolly feeling that made me more than aware that we'd had a good few bottles each the night before. We'd been talking about future plans, what we wanted to do with our lives, and for an hour or two we'd become frighteningly serious.

Today would be different. Breakfast, a hike, then hitting the village pub for lunch.

There was a stile in the corner of the huge garden that led into the neighbouring field. I climbed over and dropped into the corn, walking around the edge so as not to trample too many shoots. I entered another world. I hadn't realised how much the order of the cottage's garden had bothered me until I walked with the hedgerow to my left, thick with brambles, spotted with bloody poppies, holed here and there with rabbit warrens, rustling and whispering with secret nature that, I was sure, was far more vocal away from where I walked. I had the impression that I dragged a bubble of silence with me, a cautionary stillness that accompanied my every footfall, every breath. Perhaps if I sat and remained motionless for long enough the world would start up again around me, but that would make me feel deceitful. Nature fell quiet around me for a reason, and that reason was that I was a human being. I could hardly blame it.

So I walked, and watched, and listened, and as I reached the gate that led into the next field I saw an auburn blur to my left.

The fox must have been on the other side of the thick hedge, walking out into the gateway just as I approached. It saw me instantly, and probably heard and smelled me as well, but I've always been certain that until that moment it had been unaware of me. Maybe it had mirrored my route on the other side of the hedge. Perhaps it had paused when I paused to examine a rabbit hole, its own thoughts more basic than mine: food, meat, the chase and the catch. Then when I started again so did the fox, drawing closer to the gate that would reveal us to each other without a fear in its head. Foxes were always cautious, I knew that, especially during the day when there were farmers with shotguns and dogs. But they also had families that needed feeding. And like the farmers that despised them so, the foxes worked the land to find that food.

It felt like several minutes that we stood there staring, daring each other to make a move. I've never felt time distorted to such an extent. Whenever I look back I cannot honestly say how long we remained on either side of the open gate. I saw the fox's fur rise on its back when a breeze sang up the hillside, and a heartbeat later my fringe lifted in sympathy. Its eyes glittered. Its mouth hung open slightly, and I saw the pink tongue in there, moist and shiny as it moved ever so slightly, stretching and contracting with each fast breath. One of its ears twitched and I turned my head slightly, looking down into the fox's field to see whether there was anything else moving in there. Nothing. No cows or sheep, no farmer or hikers, no rabbits or birds. A couple of butterflies danced frantic patterns in the morning sunlight a dozen paces away, and in that moment of utter stillness and clarity of vision I fancied I could hear their delicate wings singing at the air. I saw corn shift as the sky let out its held breath, and I could almost smell it moving, sense the shifting of balance all around me as the landscape—living, breathing, watching and sensing—moved moment to moment.

I was not holding my breath. My heart pumped faster than usual, and I could hear blood flowing in my ears, but I breathed normally, long calm breaths which I hoped the fox could hear. *Stay with me*, I thought, desperate for the moment to never end.

Perhaps I spoke it. Maybe in that moment of epiphany I forgot myself, and muttered to the creature as though it were my own kind. The fox darted away down the field, keeping low and tight to the hedge leading off at right angles from the one I had followed, and within seconds all I could see of it was the occasional twitch of a corn stalk as it passed by. A few seconds more and it was gone, into the next field or the copse of trees two hundred meters down the hillside. I would likely never see it again.

For a while nature came alive around me. Birds sang, things scurried through the hedgerow, and to my left I saw the grey smudge of several rabbits emerging from their burrows. Then I turned and sighed, and that bubble of cautionary silence fell once again.

For a moment I had been a part of it all. I never forgot that feeling, and I never once experienced it again.

Everything changed that day. I became a watcher, able to appreciate what I saw for the stunning miracle it was. That was not just a robin on our bird feeder, it was a living, thinking thing, filled with instinct and blessed with its own personality, more complex and wonderful than anything mankind had ever achieved in its short history on the planet. We may have landed men on the Moon, but the creation of life was way beyond us. We explored space, the continents, the oceans, while the inner-space of our own minds remained largely unknown. For a moment, staring at that fox, I had known my place in things.

Later that day, drinking yet another bottle of Old Empire with Rob and Clive, I looked out across the fields and experienced a brief shred of total understanding at the way things worked. And though that instant terrified me so much that Clive dropped his beer and asked what was wrong, it also gave me a sense of peace that lasted most of a lifetime.

I swerve wide around a burnt-out wreck in the middle of the road, see the deer standing on the tarmac a hundred meters away, lean the other way to avoid it, over-compensate, and feel the bike slipping away from me. My hand turns the throttle as I fall and the engine screams, wheels throwing up a haze of smoke as rubber burns. I let go of the handlebars and wrap my arms around my head. In those couple of seconds between losing control and striking the ground, I realise how casual I have already become about what we are doing.

If I break a leg now, there is no hospital to go to, no doctor to set the bone, no antibiotics readily available. Only pain and suffering. I'll probably die.

I am travelling at less that fifteen miles per hour, but it's fast enough to kill me if I land wrong.

I hit the ground on my left side, skid, feel the bike go out from under me and slide on ahead, and then I begin to roll. I go over and over several times, taking the impacts on my elbows and knees, my back and hips. I come to a halt resting against the deflated tyres of a blue car, and I remain motionless. *If it hurts when I move, I could be in big trouble.*

I hear the motorbike stall as it scrapes to a halt. I open my eyes and peer between my elbows, and of course the deer is gone.

The sound of the Range Rovers' engines change and footsteps come toward me. I roll onto my back. Someone groans and I think, *Is that them? Are they groaning at what they see of my face?* But then I realise that the groan has come from me, and I let my arms drops away to my sides.

Jacqueline is first by my side, eyes darting left and right as she looks for blood or the white of broken bones. Her face relaxes as she sees neither, and she leans in and touches my face. "Are you hurt?" The others are there then, crowding around with matching looks of concern.

"Pride badly dented," I say.

"Gave me a fucking heart attack," the Irishman says. He grins down at me, lights a cigarette and looks around, as though keeping watch.

I sit up slowly, waiting for pain to kick in from cracked ribs or chipped elbows. But I've been lucky. I can feel the trickle of blood running down my left sleeve, and my trousers are torn at the knees, but I don't think there's any lasting damage. I should feel petrified, but I don't. I'm exhilarated. I'm like a speed junkie who's just had his first fix for a long time.

Something calls out from the woods to the north, a long, low moan the likes of which I've never heard before. The Irishman frowns, looks down at me, and I shrug.

"What was that?" Jessica asks.

"Fox," the Irishman says. "They can sound like babies screaming when they mate."

"Doesn't sound like a fox to me," Jessica says.

"Did you see the deer?" I ask. "It was just standing in the middle of the road. Just stood there staring at me as I came toward it, as though it knew I'd fall off."

"Didn't see a deer," Cordell says. He's gazing off across the fields, waiting for the fox—or whatever it is—to call again.

Jacqueline looks at me, touching my face, holding my hand as I go to stand.

"Is the bike okay?" the Irishman asks. It has skidded along the road, leaving white scratched streaks across the tarmac, and I sniff as we approach, expecting petrol. But it seems that the old motorbike is as hardy as me; apart from some bumps and scrapes it's in good working order. I mount it, roll forward a few feet, and smile when it kicks to life first time.

"So let's go," I say.

"But carefully," Jessica says. "We can't waste time having to bury you." She turns away without smiling and passes Cordell, where he still stands staring over the fields toward the woods.

"Didn't sound like a fox to me," Cordell says.

By the time we all gathered at the Manor there was nothing on TV or radio other than three automatic broadcasts. One radio channel played a warning to "Remain in your house with all doors and windows closed" on a continuous loop that became maddening after thirty seconds. The only TV picture was a blank screen with the words "Hold for a speech from the Prime Minister." We held for a while, then turned it off. The final radio broadcast, which one or the other of us turned on quite often before it suddenly ended three weeks after the plagues, played "Wonderful World" over and over again. Before the end of the world, that song never failed to make me cry. Afterward, Louis Armstrong's grizzled voice and wondrous lyrics inspired melancholy rather than sadness. The thing was, from what I could see from the folly up behind the Manor, it still *was* a wonderful world, though one where humanity suddenly had so much less involvement.

From the very beginning, we had all been of one mind. The Manor was stocked with food and, more importantly, a cellar full of wine and beer. We could fight our way across the shattered landscape to here or there, but none of us had knowledge that hinted at anything better elsewhere. So the alternative course of action was to remain in the Manor and see what happened. Eat. Drink. Remember.

Even Jacqueline, who professed to hating the taste of real ale, enjoyed several bottles each night after our first week together.

It was not that we were trying to shut out reality by drowning it in alcohol. That wasn't it at all. It was simply that we had much better things to remember than what was happening to us there and then. The past was a happier place, and beer was a happy way to get there.

Except for Jessica. Maybe ten years older than me, she never gave a clue about what she had lost, who she had left behind. She never actually told me outright that there was no one, but I gleaned it from her eyes, her casual acceptance, and the fact that she seemed more content than any of us with her lot.

"It's a fine day when the end of the world comes, and all you have to do is drink beer," the Irishman said one night.

I agreed with him. "Real ale apocalypse," I said. He started giggling, I laughed, and the two of us stayed up drinking until the early hours, unable to talk through our tears.

We head off again and this time I drive slower, taking more care, edging past wrecked cars and watching out for debris on the road. And deer. I *did* see it, I know that, no matter that none of the others saw. It was there, staring me out and willing me to fall, and fall I did. So much must have changed.

But it's not only newly confident animals that pose a danger. There are plenty of broken branches and leaf slicks from the winter, and here and there something larger blots the way; half a bumper from a crashed car, a Wellington boot, a crash helmet with one side caved in. I pass by a beer barrel standing on its end, one side gashed open. Soon after that there's a full bathroom suite smashed across the road—sink, toilet, bath. It's old—the bath is cast iron—and the scum stains are still visible beneath winter's slime. There are no vans or lorries close by, nothing to explain what this bathroom is doing here. And I realise that this is now a world of mystery. Before the plagues—before the end—something like this could have been investigated. Perhaps the sanitary ware carried manufacturer's codes, or even labels saying where and when it was bought or fitted. Its owners could be tracked down, and an explanation offered as to why it had ended up smashed and strewn across a dual carriageway. Now, with everyone dead, knowledge is rarer than ever before. Mystery is the order of the day. It's a wilder world we lived in, one where there doesn't always have to be a reason.

I wonder what the conversation is turning to back in the Range Rovers. We've been housebound for six months, apart from a few short, hesitant trips beyond the Manor's boundaries. Now we have given up everything we had on the word of one man, a man who came and went in the blink of an eye. I've always been guilty of self-doubt, but now it crushes in, crowding me with images of Michael's face, teasing me. I remember his smile, his frown, the way his mouth turned up at the edges when he spoke, and I remember nothing of Ashley but the tears.

I wonder if he inspires such guilt in the others. I know so little about them, really, even though we have spent weeks drinking and talking and reminiscing over old times. I know details of their past and their memories, but so little about *them*.

The road remains quite clear for the next hour, and we only have to stop once for Jacqueline to nudge a wrecked car aside with her Range Rover. Its wheels scream as it is pushed across the tarmac, deflated tyres ripping apart like torn skin.

We crest a hill and see the stain of Newport on the countryside miles ahead, the M4 motorway a textured line two miles away, and we decide to stop for something to eat and drink. We park on the side of the road behind an overturned lorry. Its doors have been forced open and a drift of orange trays has fallen from inside. They used to hold wrapped loaves of bread, but the produce has long since turned black and hard.

We sit alongside each other on the crash barrier, facing away from the road, across the drainage ditch and up a steep hillside toward the wooded summit. The trees up there seem to have welcomed spring early this year, their leaves already forming a thick canopy that captures the sun. The hillside below them is spotted with a few dead cattle long since rotted to bone and hide. Previously trim hedges have exploded into the fields, daffodils are sprinkled across the hillside like a dusting of pollen, and here and there I see clumps of shoots springing from the ground. Size is difficult to judge without anything for comparison, but the shoots seem to be at least as tall as the dead sheep lying around them. I wonder what they are—not crop plants, for sure. Jacqueline hands me an opened tin of peach halves and I begin to eat.

"We'll have to camp somewhere," Cordell says. He looks at the sky. "Way past midday already. If the M4 is relatively clear we may make the Severn before we have to stop. I don't want to travel by night."

"Why not?" Jessica asks. She's unwrapping a smoked sausage, making sure we all have a fair share of everything.

"Don't know what's out here," he says. And he's right.

We all know that, because none of us questions him.

"Maybe we could use a hotel," I say. "Or pull off and find an old pub, kip down there."

"Maybe."

We eat, enjoying the sun on the backs of our necks and the good food. Jessica opens a bottle of wine and we have a small glass each. I almost decline—I'm riding a motorbike after all. But a couple of mouthfuls won't do me any harm. I smile at her, offer my thanks, and Cordell says, "What the *fuck* is *that?*"

A large shape is moving across the hillside, high up, almost at the level of the trees. It's huge, and for a second or two I think I see long segmented legs stretching out, limbs forcing it along, clawed feet ripping out clods of earth and flinging them aside. Then I blink and remember falling from the motorbike, and I know what we're looking at.

"Deer," I say. "A herd of deer."

"Here?" Jessica asks. She knows nature, and she knows we shouldn't be seeing what we are.

I shrug. "It's been six months…"

The deer are running across the hill, keeping close to the woods yet seemingly reticent about going inside. They surely can't hear, see or smell us from this far away, and our vehicles would blend in with the dozens of other cars and trucks stopped along this stretch of road.

So I wonder what it is that has them spooked.

"We could take a shot at them," Cordell says. "Damn, you fancy a nice venison dinner, guys?"

"You'll never get close enough," Jessica says. She stands slowly, shields her eyes with her hand. "They're not supposed to be here," she says quietly, almost to herself.

Something comes out of the woods. A darting grey shape, soon joined by three more. They spread out around the flock of deer, which flows and pulses like a flock of birds dancing across the sky.

Jacqueline gasps.

"What?" Cordell says. "What now?"

"Dogs gone feral," Jacqueline says. "Must be thousands of them out in the wild now. And cats."

"And budgies, tortoises and goldfish," the Irishman says.

"Not dogs." Jessica is leaning forward as though to see better. "Damn!" Quiet again, as though talking to herself, and I feel my patience wearing.

"Jessica, what are you seeing?" I say.

She glances at me, and I see a glint in her eyes. She's not afraid, not shocked. She's *excited*.

"Wolves," she says. "I'm seeing wolves!"

Cordell laughs, an uncertain cough that sums up what we're all thinking.

"They were talking about breeding them in Scotland, weren't they?" Jacqueline asks. "Letting them out in the wild up there? In a protected preserve?"

"Talking about it, yes," Jessica agrees. "But it never happened. Too many objections from local farmers and people who thought the wolves would carry off their babies."

"So…" I say.

"So, where have those come from?"

We watch the shapes darting back and forth around the

herd of deer, trying to drive them up toward the woods. The wolves—if that's really what they are—are very spare in their movements. There's no exuberant barking or howling, no running around in circles. They move only when they have to, and within another couple of minutes the deer are rustling the bushes that grow around the trunks of the first trees.

That's when they spring the trap.

We can't see clearly from this far away, but it's obvious that more wolves have been waiting under cover. When the deer are close enough they leap, and then the animals guarding the herd dart in to join the kill. The deer scatter, run and then regroup, fleeing northward even though they are no longer being chased.

Several of their kind have been left behind. They struggle briefly, buried beneath the grey shapes, and I hear a faint cry. And then silence. Several wolves back away from the sudden red splash on the hillside and lie down, waiting their turn.

"Leader of the pack," Jessica says. "Damn, I've read about this but never thought…"

"Never thought you'd see it in Britain," Cordell finished for her.

"Maybe they were pets that got out," Jessica muses.

"Are you sure they're wolves?" I ask. "Not dogs? Alsatians?"

She shakes her head, very definite.

"Well, my vote is that we move on," Jacqueline says. Out of all of us, she's the only one who really looks afraid.

Later, I will begin to wonder whether she had an inkling of what was going on, even then. Perhaps Michael had told her more than anyone else because he saw how quiet she was, how attuned to the dangers around her. She drank less than anyone, and thought more. I believe she had a past she did not wish to revisit, and memories for her were as intimidating as the plagues were for everyone else.

But by the time I get around to thinking about this, it's far too late. By then Jacqueline is dead, and we're beginning to know the truth.

SIX

LONDON PRIDE

On a hot day in the capital, interspersed with pints of London Pride—hoppy, with a citrus bite and a light bitter finish—whenever we could find a pub not jammed to the gills with thirsty marchers and press people eager for a drink, Ashley and I joined a protest march against the war in Iraq. It was an adventure. We'd travelled down the night before, enjoying the communal spirit on the coach, Ashley dozing with her head resting against my shoulder, slowing as we neared London and taking four hours to make our eventual way, snake-like, into the city. We had intended staying in a guest house that night, but it was almost three a.m. by the time we poured from the bus. We thanked the exhausted driver and he smiled back, giving us a cheerful peace sign and telling us to go get them. Once on the street we found that the atmosphere was already buzzing. Hundreds of people were dipping in and out of all night diners, with many more pitching stands and tables from which they were selling banners, placards and tee-shirts.

"Shall we hit the sack?" I asked.

"I don't think I could sleep a wink!" Ashley said. She grasped my hand and we plunged into the crowd. She'd been asleep for four hours on the coach and I'd grabbed barely half an hour, but I was so thrilled by her enthusiasm that I didn't have the heart to insist.

And I'm glad I didn't. We ate an early breakfast—or a very late supper—of sausages, mash and onion gravy, then found a pub that was probably breaking a dozen laws by being open at four in the morning. Trade was manic, and the landlord seemed to enter into the spirit of safe rebellion by halving the prices of his drinks. We settled down at a small corner table and drank London Pride at less than two pounds per pint. It was bliss. We could barely hear each other talk above the hubbub, but we spent much of the time listening to the good-natured banter, the occasional song, and the exhortations of a tall Scot who insisted on dancing on tables and regaling us with poems no one could understand.

The Pride was gorgeous. I'd drank it outside London but it never seemed to travel very well. Perhaps it didn't like being away from home. Here it was smooth and rich, giving a distinct hoppy smell and a full-bodied taste. The pub served its beer in mugs, which was a refreshing change, and by the time the march was due to start at nine a.m. we'd already had several pints, some more food, and a couple of hours of lively singing, chanting and cheering.

When we exited the pub and headed north toward the

march, we passed a group of more serious protestors standing on the corner. We were here because we felt bad about the war, the lies spewing from politicians' mouths, the whole basis upon which we were invading another country. It made Ashley and me angry and we'd printed our own "Not in My Name" tee-shirts, because we didn't want some side-street vendor profiting from such heartfelt conviction.

These people standing on the corner had built a screen from torn cardboard boxes and timber framing. They'd covered its entire surface with white paper and then started affixing pictures, photographs and bold lines of quoted rhetoric at various places. George Bush, Tony Blair, Saddam Hussein, military hardware, oil drilling rigs, the UN flag, the French President, soldiers with brown skin and white, a group of children playing in a park in London, a group of children playing in a park in Baghdad. When they'd finished they connected faces with words, images with photographs, and then they combined the disparate threads and joined them at the centre. There sat a gruesome photograph from the first Gulf War, showing the effects of a high-explosive bomb on the confined space of a bomb shelter. Written across the temporary screen below this photograph, in what I was almost certain must have been one of the protestor's blood, was the word *Innocent*.

The crowd grew quiet as it passed this presentation. A few still bickered and jeered, but mostly we were cowed by the seriousness of the display. We were here partly for the protest, but mostly for ourselves, pandering to some deep-felt guilt and trying to give ourselves a sense of having done something positive. We were being safe, and hoping it would make a difference.

The display shamed me in ways it should not have. It made me sad that we'd been drinking beer and having fun while these protestors faced such dreadful photographs, pinned them up, cut their veins to add their words of defiance.

"How can they be so *intense?*" Ashley said to me. "It's all about a combined voice, isn't it? We're here in numbers, not to see who can be most horrifying." And she was right. We passed the make-do display board and its creators, leaving them in a bubble of uncomfortable silence that hung in many places across London that day. Mostly the people on the march were like us, ready for a day out to make our voice heard and our statistic felt. Ashley and I did not feel bad about that. We marched, wore our tee-shirts, and we even got to speak into a camera from a regional TV station in Wales, though we never found out whether the interview was broadcast.

Indeed, some of these more extreme protestors tended to spoil the spirit of the day. One group of them chanted, "Blair fucks Bush!" again and again, unconcerned at the presence of young kids brought along by their parents to take part in this public outpouring of opinion. Another started a shuffling, clumsy scuffle with police, and while they were handcuffed and led away they shouted about fascist abuse and the stifling of freedom of speech. We looked and shook our heads, because we were as free as anyone. We were making our feelings felt. We were *saying* something, and doing so far more effectively than being locked away in the back of a police van.

The sense of camaraderie was powerful and dizzying, and there was no impatience whilst queuing for food or toilets, no anger, no tempers flaring. Ashley and I sat outside a pub drinking London Pride late that afternoon, our feet sore and legs aching from walking so far, and a gang of kids from a school in Yorkshire put on an impromptu acrobatic display in the street while their teachers enjoyed a drink.

"They'll remember this forever," one of the teachers said to me, sipping from his drink, his eyes alight.

"Do you think it'll do any good?" I asked.

He shook his head. "Absolutely not. But it never was about stopping the war, was it?"

I thought about that for a long time, and later when Ashley and I were making love in our guest house bedroom, I knew what he meant. We marched, but we knew it would never stop the war. We made love, but we knew now that we could never have children. It was the process that made a difference, not the end effect, and it was all about love. Afterwards I told her what I thought, and she agreed.

"Not hippyish, not Seventies-flowers-in-our-hair," she said, "but yes, today was all about love." We held each other close as we fell asleep, happy that we had made a difference.

Cordell offers to ride the bike but I refuse. It already feels like mine. We have ridden and fallen together, and in truth there's something special about it because it was Michael's. *And whose before his?* I think. *Whose was this bike before Michael found it coughing away alone, by the side of the road?* Cordell claps me on the shoulder and tells me to take care.

We head down the hill toward the M4 junction, and the wolves are on my mind. We just witnessed a wolf pack make a killing in the South Wales countryside. Even with everything that has happened that instils a sense of amazement in me, and I'm glad I can still feel that way. I keep glancing in my wing mirror, expecting to see loping grey shapes keeping pace with us in the fields, darting from cover to cover as they stalk us southward. Instinct goes so far, but these creatures knew what they were doing. They were practised, their assault perfected. They were wild. Our view would have been the envy of any wildlife cameraman, and though the attack was far away, still the tactics were clear.

Perhaps they'd escaped from Longleat or some other safari park when the end came. The wolves there were kept out in the open, a large enclosure where they could wander away from the fascinated gaze of children if the mood so took them. Ashley and I had been there several times (and she must have smiled, she must have *laughed*, but still I only remember her when I'm drunk). But the wolves' food at Longleat was delivered already dead, because it was felt that visitors could be disturbed to see the majestic creatures hunting and killing their own prey. Yes, instinct went so far, but I was unsure whether animals reared and kept in such surroundings could ever really adapt to the wild.

And certainly not this quickly.

Perhaps they had been living in the wild for decades. Britain echoed with these stories, tales of cryptozoology featuring wild cats and bears and wolves, and there were many professional scientists prepared to risk their reputations by agreeing with such tales. And Wales had always been a hub of sightings. With its mountain ranges and wide swathes of sparsely populated countryside, it was a natural home for creatures that wished to exist below the radar, popping up only now and then to slaughter half a flock of sheep or gash some over-inquisitive rambler's legs.

I think of the pack circling the deer, herding them, and the waiting wolves pouncing from the cover of trees. And a shiver runs down my back. I am suddenly certain that we have just witnessed something far removed from how the world was before the plagues came.

We come to a slew of wrecked vehicles, and beside the road I see the remains of a military helicopter. The rotors are clearly visible farther out in the field, detached but protruding from the ground like giant darts. The body of the aircraft is lying on its side down the embankment and across the ditch, burnt out and showing its charred metallic skeleton to the sun. Some of the crashed cars are similarly blackened, and I wonder how many people died here as a result of watching the helicopter plummet from the sky and explode. Dozens, probably. Even though billions are dead, such numbers still have more of an effect on me. A dozen is easier to imagine than a billion. I can see a dozen faces from my life, but a billion is beyond my comprehension.

There's a skeleton on the road. I see it at the last minute, thinking that it was a shred of cloth or a scrap of tattered cardboard, and I ride across it, wincing as the bones crush beneath my wheels. I look left and right at the shattered cars, trying not to wonder whose son or husband, daughter or mother I have just run over. *Roadkill*, I think, and the image does not sit well.

Something has come this way since the accident. I'm riding across wide swathes of melted tarmac where burning cars had once stood, but now they're piled at crazy angles along the side of the road, torn bodies huddled together against prying eyes. Lucky for us, otherwise the Range Rovers would never make it through. I wonder who it was, and when, and what they had been driving. I hope that the cleared route continues.

We're drawing closer to the large roundabout below the motorway flyover. And this is where our whole journey could change. If the motorway is jammed with abandoned vehicles then we will have to walk, and a trip that would take perhaps two days in vehicles would stretch to weeks on foot. *Can we really walk that far?* I think. *With everything that might be out there, can we go that far without meeting something or someone dangerous, or succumbing to hunger or thirst, or just giving up?* It's not a thought I wish to explore at any length, nor a situation I want to experience.

Right now, I could kill a pint of beer. Bluebird Ale from Coniston Brewery sticks in my head for some reason, a beer I have not seen for sale in many places. *Drinking atoms of Donald Campbell with every mouthful*, Ashley had once said, displaying the gruesome streak of humour she mostly kept in check. But it was a good beer, and we shared good times drinking it, and for a moment faster than the blink of an eye Ashley smiles at me and sees away the fears.

There's something else marring the surface of the road ahead. I frown and squint, sure that the sun is dazzling me and perhaps setting a mirage in my path. The road seems heavily textured, bubbled and spiked, and I roll to a stop. The vehicles halt behind me, and I hear the expectant purr of their motors. I hold up one hand and roll slowly forward.

The stretch of road is clear, so it's not somewhere scorched by a blazing car. There are no bodies, no debris on the tarmac, and then colour crowds in and I know what I'm seeing.

Shoots. Thousands of them, thin and sharp and spiked with bright green leaves yet to unfurl. Most of them have barely broken the surface of the road, but some are several inches high, thick at the base and pointed at the top. A few —maybe two dozen—would probably reach my knee, and these have started to spread and sprout now that they're free of the ground. I don't recognise them. The heads of these taller specimens have fattened leaves spreading from the bulbous tops and seeking the sun.

Trees? I'm not sure. I edge forward and kick out at a couple of the shorter shoots, snapping them off. Their exposed cores glitter wet in the sunlight. They've forced their way up through the road across a wide area, extending from here all the way down to the motorway roundabout. They're small, weak plants, and yet for some reason I feel reticent about riding through them.

Jacqueline toots her horn and I glance back. She's leaning from the window, hand outstretched as if to say, *What?* I shake my head, shrug and move on.

I cannot feel the shoots snapping beneath the motorcycle's wheels, but I know they are. I cannot even hear them breaking beneath the much wider tyres of the Range Rovers. We plough through this new spread of greenery and growth, leaving behind us the scars of our journey in crushed lines of life, and we don't even notice what we are doing.

We have seen no one else alive. There have been plenty of bodies in sealed cars, charred skeletons on the roadside, vague humps at the edges of fields bordering the road that could have been the remains of people fleeing something in the traffic. But we are the only living humans here. I feel like an intruder in this world, and I have already berated myself for thinking of it as a dead place. It's far from dead. Bereft of humanity, maybe, but perhaps all the more alive because of that. Birds flock and flicker through the air, and here and there I've seen the distinctive gatherings of stick and feather nests, resting in the arms of blackened bent metal along the road. There were the wolves a couple of miles back, and other large shapes move across the fields. Foxes, I'm guessing, and more deer, and perhaps cattle that managed to survive the winter and are now reaping the green benefits of spring. The roar of our engines startles some shapes into stillness, but others seem unconcerned at our passing. A family of rabbits sits beside the road and watches us drive past, eyeing the Range Rover wheels suspiciously.

High above, I see two huge birds circling. Buzzards, perhaps, though they look too large for that. *Eagles*, I think. But that's ridiculous. There are some wild eagles left in the northern reaches of Scotland, but…

But what about the wolves?

As I start slowing toward the motorway roundabout I see the unmistakeable outline of a person walking from west to east along the overpass. The shape pauses, looks our way and begins to run.

"So why are we still alive?" Cordell asked. It was our fourth night at the Manor, and the first night we were all there together. Jessica had come in that day, cycling down the lane and spotting me standing on the folly's balcony. She had stopped and zinged her bicycle bell, waved, and turned in the gates. I had smiled, delighted at the innocence of such a gesture. Humanity lay dead and rotting around us, and here was this woman, riding her bike and waving as though she was on a summer bike ride before lunch. It was the first time I'd smiled in almost a week.

"Don't know," the Irishman said. "Maybe we've all got something in common. Something in our blood. Makes us immune. I'm a Celt, what about you lot?" He smiled at Cordell, who scowled back.

"No need for that," Jacqueline said.

"I'm jesting with you, that's all," the Irishman said. "I'll not take the piss unless I like someone, and I like you all. How's that, then? I'm not the easiest to please, when it comes to meeting new folks. I'm stubborn and I don't suffer fools gladly."

"No fools here," I said.

"You're right!" the Irishman said. "No fools here. Five of us, and no fools."

Jessica tapped her beer bottle with her wedding band, frowning. "I've been thinking about this a lot," she said. "I've cycled maybe a hundred miles since the end, across South Wales and through the Brecon Beacons, and I've not seen anyone else. No one. I was really beginning to think I was the only one left alive, and I tried to understand why, and I came up with the idea that maybe I was dead. Dead, and haunting the mountains. And maybe everyone else was dead too, and they were haunting other places. Or the very same places, but I just couldn't see them. Maybe everyone haunts their own version of the world."

"Six billion worlds to haunt," Jacqueline muttered.

"Well, I'm not dead," Cordell said. He leaned across and punched the Irishman on the arm. "Dead?"

"Not me." The Irishman took another swig of his beer. "Damn, that'd taste nowhere near as good if I were."

"Something in our past?" I said. "I had whooping cough when I was a kid. Got a steel rod in my wrist from where I fell off a skateboard."

"I had meningitis," Cordell said.

"So did I!" Jacqueline said.

Jessica shook her head. "I've always been very healthy. Colds and bugs, and aches and pains as I get older, but I've never had what I'd class as an *illness*."

"Perhaps that's it," I said. "We're all unusually fit and healthy."

"I had breast cancer," Jacqueline said. "Five years ago."

We sat silently for a while, and all five of us took a drink at exactly the same time.

"So are you all clear?" Cordell asked.

Jacqueline nodded, smiling. I liked the expression on her face right then, but it would be so rare.

"Maybe it was something we ate," the Irishman said. He snorted, took a drink and started laughing, spitting his beer across the table. We joined in, and we ended up having a good evening. From then on we gave up trying to fathom why we seemed to be the only survivors of the human race.

No fools here, I said. And I was right, none of us were fools.

The people we meet on the slip road up to the M4 *are* fools. So that's that theory blown out of the water. They're fools because the first thing they do is reach for their guns.

And then they start shooting.

It takes me a few seconds to realise that the shots are wild and panicked, but I also know that they've got more than air rifles and shotguns. I've only ever heard automatic weapons fired in movies, but the angry rattle is obvious, and I feel bullets hailing past my head as I fall from the bike. I protect my head, roll, and drag myself to the side of the road. I stop when I hear the ping and crack of bullets striking metal. I've come to rest behind an overturned car, and I sit up and look back down the slip-road.

Jessica and Cordell have already driven below the overpass, out of the shooters' line of sight.

Great idea, I think. *Great idea of mine. Drive up on my*

own to show we're not a threat. Fucking great.

I was still a hundred meters from the road block when they started shooting, but I'd seen enough. There was a heavy pick-up truck and an ambulance parked across the road, a double-decker bus head-on between them, and beyond that several caravans and four-wheel drives. The shooting came from the upper deck of the bus.

Down the road, Cordell peers cautiously around the corner of the bridge. I raise my hand—not too far—and he nods.

The silence is shocking after the thunderous gunshots. My bike has stalled, and the only sound is the idling motors of the Range Rovers out of sight beneath the motorway. Maybe they are already planning on how to get me away from here... but I hope not. The shooting had started wild and it missed me, but the shooters have had time to gather their senses. And the Rovers are much larger targets.

Cordell glances around again and I wave him away. Shake my hands, shake my head, trying to convey my thoughts: *Don't come up this way.* He nods and disappears again, and I hope he understood.

"Hello in the bus!" I shout. There is no response. No more shooting, and no answering shouts.

Are they circling around to me now? Crawling along the ditch to my right, or up on the motorway bridge to my left? I look up at the road barrier, expecting to see a head and gun peering over at any minute. There's no way they would miss from up there. I could run, I suppose, and trust that their inexperience would not let them hit a moving target. But it's not a scenario that offers much comfort. I don't want to die with my brains splattered across warm tarmac. I don't want the others to see me shot down, and leave me as they drive in the opposite direction. I don't want to be just another fading memory in their tired minds.

"Hello in the bus!" I shout again, trying to inject some urgency into my voice. My only answer is a metallic clatter and a curse. The only blessing is that it sounded as though it had come from the road block, and not closer.

I look up and see a flock of birds making patterns against the blue sky. It's a big flock, and I'm not sure I've ever seen so many birds together before. Swifts, I think. Picking flies from the air, or maybe communicating in some way I cannot imagine.

"See the birds?" I shout. "I'm as harmless as them. We're not here for trouble, and we don't want to hurt you."

The gun cracks in again, and a dozen bullets rip into the car or ricochet from its flaking shell. I roll into a ball and pray I'm hiding in the best place. The shooting fades away to stunned silence once more, and I find no holes in my body. *Holy shit*, I think, *I'm being shot at!* My jacket is grubby, and the white shirt beneath has picked up a heavy smear of oil from somewhere. I think of Bruce Willis and begin to giggle. That's not good. Giggling to myself when someone's trying to blow my guts across South Wales… that's not good.

I glance downhill and Cordell is there, peering up at me and waiting for me to move. I raise a hand again and he nods and disappears. He'd been carrying the shotgun that time.

"Fuck's sake!" I shout, and it's a sudden sense of panic more than an attempt at communication.

"Stand up!" a voice shouts.

"And have you blow my head off?"

"I can't hit the side of a barn, old man."

"I'm forty-five! I'm not old."

"You're bald!"

"I was bald when I was eighteen!" My face is pressed close to the tarmac and I can see ants marching in a line. Some of them carry pine needles, others carry dead ants. They're larger than any wood ants I have ever seen, and I wonder where their nest may be.

"So stand up!"

"Are you going to shoot?"

"Are you going to eat us?"

Eat? I frown, shake my head. Did he really say that? "*Eat* you?"

Silence, and then some muffled voices. I hear a clang of metal on metal again, and then a motor starts uphill from me.

I freeze. Listen. It sounds like a big diesel engine, perhaps the bus. If they choose to drive down and ram the car I'm hiding behind I'll be squashed flat. The ants march on before my nose, and I know that they'll survive.

I look down the gently sloping road. I *could* run, but it's a long couple of hundred meters. Plenty of time for a bad shot to get lucky.

The engine rattles as it's revved. Cordell looks around the bridge footing again, shakes his head, raises his hands palm-up, and I have no idea what he's trying to say.

I risk a look around the end of the overturned car and don't get my head blown off. It's difficult to see which vehicle has been started, but there's activity on the bus. The sun is glaring from its windscreen, so I can't see whether or not there's anyone in the driver's seat.

I'm starting to sweat. The sun is hitting the car and melting onto me, and the coat I wore to ride the bike is suddenly too hot. For the first time I turn and try to see inside the car, but its roof is crushed down on my side, and a slick of broken glass and ripped interior shields my view. It doesn't smell of anything too bad. I hope it's empty.

Either side of me are several places where bullets have blasted through its metal shell. My blood runs cold.

I stand up. There's really nothing else I can do. Run and they'll shoot me for sure, stay here and they'll ram the car and crush me into the road. Stand, submit, and perhaps they'll keep fingers from triggers long enough for us to talk.

I raise my arms and wait for the shot. It does not come. Nobody shouts either, and I begin to wonder where they've gone.

"Quickly!" It's a distant shout, and I turn and see Cordell gesturing me toward him.

"This way," another voice says. The voice with the gun. I obey, stepping out from behind the car and walking slowly toward the barricade. As I walk I have time to take in more details, and none of it fills me with hope. The pick-up truck has been there for a long time, because its tyres are flat and there's a swathe of rust spotting its heavy hood. Its windscreen is smashed. The ambulance looks as though it could be mobile, but its rear doors are pressed hard against the retaining wall holding back the motorway twenty feet above. Its cab is ridged and dented, and rough sheets of metal have been welded across its windows. Between the truck and the ambulance is the bus, and as I move closer I can see it moving slightly as people walk about inside. Its engine growls. The front window is missing upstairs, and a man and woman are hunkered down, guns protruding over the sill and tracking my progress.

The bus is pocked with bullet holes. The driver's windscreen is hazed. For some reason they've decided not to knock it out.

"There's no harm in me," I call. I open my raised hands as though to prove I'm not carrying an unpinned hand grenade, or a vial of botulism. "We just want to come through."

"Walk to the front of the bus, put your hands on the grille and stay still," the woman shouts. I do as I'm told. I can see the shape in the driver's seat now, and I'm sure it's just a kid.

I hear the thump-thump of someone running downstairs, and seconds later the hot barrel of a gun is pressed against my temple. "Really," the man says, "don't move."

We stand there in uncomfortable silence for a few seconds. It's almost ridiculous. I wonder whether he's waiting for me to make a move so he can claim self-defence when he kills me. I don't give him the pleasure.

This is unreal, I think again, and I smile.

"What's so fucking funny?" There's fear in his voice, and I don't like that. It's dangerous.

"Sorry," I say. "I've never been shot at before. It's just all a bit surreal."

"Surreal," the man says. He snorts, then giggles. "Lucy! He thinks this is surreal."

"Tell me about it," a voice says from above. The woman, probably leaning out and covering me with her own weapon.

"Look, we don't mean any harm. We just want to get by."

"Well, you have to pay us," the man says, and for the first time I really recognise the utter terror in his voice. I wonder what he was before the plagues: a teacher? Butcher? Accountant? Lorry driver? Now the world has ended and he's just trying to survive, and I'm certain that this is the first time he's asked someone for payment to pass. *Just set up here?* I think. *Or has no one come this way in months?*

"What do you want?" I say.

"Food."

"And booze," Lucy says.

The man snorts again. "Food. Weapons, if you have any."

I don't want to reveal how pathetically armed we are. "We have some food you can have," I say.

"And booze, Billy," Lucy says again.

"Some wine."

"Okay, then," the man, Billy, says. "Okay. Tell your people to come up."

"How?"

He hesitates, then shoves the barrel of the gun hard against my head. Bad move, I think. Don't show him up, not in front of his Lucy. He needs to be in charge.

"Call them!" he says. "Tell them to come on foot."

I turn. Cordell is peering around the corner of the underpass, and I see Jessica standing just behind him. They're both holding their guns. I wave them to me, and they disappear back around the corner.

"Now we see how much they think they need you," Billy says. His gun is pointing at my gut, but his eyes are everywhere else. Checking the fields, the road above… everywhere.

"What are you scared of?" I ask.

Billy glares at me. "As if you didn't know."

He's talking about something very particular, a definite threat rather than just the wilds we have already seen. I decide to say nothing.

Cordell and the others appear around the corner and start up the incline. They're still carrying their guns, and to begin with I think Billy will go mad. But I see him size up our meagre weaponry; a shotgun, an air rifle. He and Lucy are obviously much more heavily armed, and he seems to draw power from this.

"Break the shotgun!" Billy calls. "Carry the pea shooter by the barrel." Cordell and Jessica comply. When they're twenty paces away Billy calls, "Far enough."

We stand that way for a while, silent, listening to the rumble of the bus's engine. I can sense the shape in the driver's seat behind me, its foot resting on the gas.

We all wait for someone else to speak.

"Who are you?" Cordell says at last.

"The man with the gun," Billy says.

The Irishman snickers, puts his hand over his mouth to hide his smile.

"What?" Billy demands. He moves forward one step, raising the gun. I could tackle him now. But the results of such a rash move are beyond contemplation. However bad Lucy's shooting may be, she'd cut us all down with one long burst.

"Sorry," the Irishman says. "But 'the man with the gun'…? Reminds me of a bad Steven Seagal movie I saw once."

"Was there a good one?" Lucy asks.

Billy turns and looks up at her, scowl breaking into a smile.

This is Monty Python, I think.

Jacqueline takes the initiative and, with a few words, breaks the thin ice we have all been treading. "I don't suppose you have anywhere I could pee?"

"We've been here about six months," Billy says ten minutes later. They've stopped the bus and led us behind it, into a compound formed beside the road. It has the pick-up truck on one side, a dozen sand-filled barrels forming another wall, and a heavy steel storage container closes it off from the road. It's in the container that they have made their home. Billy will not let us inside.

The bus driver turns out to be a girl of about seven or eight. She doesn't speak. Lucy says she has not spoken since they found her, days after the end, cowering in the middle of the motorway beside the bodies of her parents.

"Why not a house somewhere?" Cordell asks.

Billy nods at the bus. "We have that. We travel around quite a bit, looking for stuff. But back here feels safe. And we're waiting for someone."

"Who?"

"My son," Billy says.

"And my daughter," Lucy adds.

"Why wait here?" I ask.

"Last time I spoke to him, when the plagues were hot, Nathan said he'd try to make it here," Billy says. "It's on the way to London. Where my parents live. Nathan loves his grandparents. And I can't… I can't remember him. So he must still be alive."

"So how do you work that one out?" the Irishman says.

Billy glares at him. "If he was dead, he'd be alive in my memories."

The Irishman nods, but thankfully he realises it's best not to probe any more.

The little girl is sitting on a sand barrel, looking the other way.

"So you've set up a toll road," I say.

Billy nods.

"Many takers?" Jessica asks.

Billy's face darkens and he turns away. He seems to be staring at the ambulance.

"We'll give you some food," I say. "And we have a few bottles of wine to spare. But…"

"We can't go into Newport," Lucy says, pre-empting my question. "No way. Can't. Wouldn't. And most of the houses in the countryside seem to be occupied by… the dead. A lot of people out here went home to die."

"But all the cars on the road?" Jessica says.

"People fleeing the city. And that's why we can't go in."

"I locked them in the ambulance," Billy says suddenly. "There were only two of them. But they were… well, you know. I can *see* you know. Even after we shot them we knew they'd be up, so I dragged them into the ambulance and parked it there."

"*We* did it," Lucy says.

Cordell goes to speak but I shake my head. There is much more here than we know, but to reveal our ignorance would lose us any small advantage we may have. Billy's gun is pointing at the ground, but he still grasps it tight. It would be foolish for us to assume that we are anything more than prisoners.

"Why don't you burn it?" I ask, trying to get Billy to reveal more.

He grins at me. Shakes his head. "Very good," he says. "But no. Because now I've got my own weapons of mass destruction."

Jacqueline is terrified, I can see that. Shivering, moaning. She broke the tension earlier but she's raising it again now. Lucy is staring at her, and Billy glances at her several times before raising his gun again.

"So why are you on the road?" Lucy asks.

"Going somewhere," Cordell says.

"Where?"

"Away from where we were." I have no intention of mentioning Bar None, or Michael, or any of the ideas we have about what is happening.

"What's wrong with where you were?"

I think of what they have said, how they've acted. I look at the battered ambulance. "The things," I say.

Billy's eyes widen. "What were they like? How did they look?"

I frown and stare down at my feet.

He grunts. "I understand. Rather not say. Rather not talk about them. I understand."

And it's as easy as that.

The young girl stands and leads Jacqueline back down the ramp. She is carrying a pistol tucked into the belt of her jeans. Jacqueline walks with her head down, holding her arms and shaking. When they drive back up in one of the Range Rovers Billy reverses the bus and makes room for them to come through.

Lucy and Jessica negotiate over some food and a few bottles of wine and, our passage paid, we're given the go-ahead to retrieve the bike and the other Range Rover.

They leave us with the shotgun and air rifle, and we go on our way.

"If he was dead, he'd be alive in my memories," Billy said. I think on this as I guide the motorbike slowly along the motorway. *"Alive in my memories."*

Ashley is dead in my memories. Unless I take a drink and let taste and texture inspire the past, she is a blank where she should be whole, a void where she should be the heaviest thing in my mind. If she was dead I'd be carrying her still, but I feel more empty than I ever have before.

"Billy is mad," I mutter at the breeze. "And Lucy. Both of them mad." And I think of the ambulance with its back doors pressed tight against the concrete wall, metal welded and bolted over the windows, dents in its sides as though made by something inside trying to get out.

I'm approaching another exit from the motorway, this one leading into the heart of Newport along Caermaen Road. I have travelled this road so often with Ashley. I can see her crying and dying, see her lying dead on her bed, but can I really? I was almost mad myself by then; insane with the cries and wailing of my dying neighbours, the smell of my sick wife, and the impossibility of my own unblemished skin, clear lungs, hopeful, crazy eyes. Can I really trust my own memories of that final time so much?

The exit is close now, a couple of hundred meters away. I ease down on the throttle. Our house is less than a mile from here, in a nice cul-de-sac close to the centre of town. The area had been improved drastically in the years before the plagues. Pedestrianised streets, housing grants, parks, planting. It was a nice place to live.

Ashley could still be there.

I saw her die, I saw her tears and pain and I can still *see them, even now.*

Nevertheless, I cannot feel the weight of my wife's history inside. And she had meant so much to me that her death would surely be heavy indeed.

Knowing that I was mad to listen to a madman, still Billy's words had affected me. If I applied them to myself they answered some questions, but they presented twice as many. These new questions—Is she dead? Is she alive? Is she still here?—could be answered so much more easily. A turn of the handlebars. A ten minute diversion. Proof, of what I thought I knew.

"A mile from here," I say, and I turn from the motorway.

There's a chorus of horns behind me. I know I should stop and explain, but to do so would be to allow Jessica and the others to talk me out of this. She is wise and I feel weak, and I would end up in the back of a Range Rover while the Irishman rode the bike closer and closer to Bar None. And I would be as safe as could be then, but I'd never know. I'd have to watch the last of Newport fading behind us, never to be seen again. And even if I closed my eyes… still only the tears of death.

"Sorry!" I shout. I wave a hand, trying to communicate that I won't be long. In my side mirrors I see Cordell flashing lights and the Irishman hanging from the passenger window, waving as though to haul me back. They follow me, and I feel an instant stab of guilt. *They don't want to leave me behind.*

This exit ramp rises to a roundabout above the motorway, and at the top of the ramp there's a knot of cars tied together by the ghost of a terrible fire. Their shells have been melted into grotesque shapes, spiked ribs and metallic spines that look for all the world like the skeletons of living things. I can squeeze by, just, and as I use my feet to guide the motorbike through the narrowest of gaps, that guilt punches in again.

I can't look back. I hear the Range Rovers stop, the doors open, voices calling out in confusion and dismay, and I can't look back.

I pause, leaning to one side to support the bike. "My house!" I call. "I have to see. Just to make sure. To make certain my certainty. You understand?"

"No!" the Irishman says. "You're a fucking idiot, and I don't understand a word!"

"I understand," Jacqueline says. I still can't turn, but I smile. And I really believe she does.

"You'll get yourself killed!" Jessica shouts.

Cordell joins in. "The city's not safe, you know that, Michael told us, everything's wrong and rotten and…"

"Give him half an hour," Jacqueline says. "Please?"

"Half an hour," I shout. Without waiting for a reply—a yes or a no—I rev the bike and move away.

And I don't, I *can't*, look back.

I'm not sure what I expected. Streets filled with marauding zombies, maybe. The hate-filled dead rising up at my impertinence, clawing their way through closed wooden doors, rising from hastily dug graves, reaching for me with nails crusted with the dried blood of older victims. Or groups of pet dogs gone feral, Alsatians leading packs of corgis, a King Labrador ruling over a domain of vicious poodles, terriers and spaniels. Maybe I'd expected to see half the town in ruins, fallen victim to pyromaniacs and vandals since society's rapid decline. All the clichés.

But I see none of these. There is damage, of course, and plenty of signs that things are not right. The first row of houses lining Caermaen Road is scarred by a rubble-filled gap, as though time has punched out one of the town's teeth. Gas explosion, I guess. Front gardens have gone wild, carefully maintained borders swallowed by tangle root, and lawns are lush and heavy. And here and there, the remains of bodies.

The main impression I get as I ride closer to my old house is that everyone has gone away, and what they left behind will take its time to die. This is what Armageddon has always looked like in my mind's eye. It means the end of humanity, not the end of the world. I'd dreamed this once as a teenager: an empty world, humanity gone or been taken, and its roads and paths, rooms and gardens slowly being overtaken by nature once again. In five years there will be no sign of these carefully maintained gardens. Ten years from now the roads and pavements will be turned crazy by roots and shoots breaking through from below. In twenty years some of the roofs will fail, forty years walls will fall, and a century from now this will be a forgotten city. Animals will own it once again. There will be rooms that survive, and places where the stain of humanity will take much longer to be cleaned away. But it won't take forever.

It's sad, but I can't help thinking of it as something of a triumph.

Maybe I really am mad, I think, and then I turn the corner into my own cul-de-sac.

Memories rush in. In all of them Ashley is a presence but not an image.

"Be there," I say, but there's no way she can. Even if the grey area of my memory *is* fooling me, and she *didn't* die, there would be no reason for her to remain in our home. There had been none for me.

"I left because you were dead," I say. I switch off the bike and kick down the stand. The silence is shattering. The last revs echo away between houses and back along the street, and then I am in a silence broken only by the breath of the wind. There are birds, but they sing in the distance. I guess that anything nearby has been shocked into muteness by my appearance.

I remain motionless, breathing as gently as fear and anticipation will allow, until the birds start singing again. They flit from roof to roof, disappearing into eaves and through the eyes of smashed windows. They bring life to this place, and I hope, I pray, that they're an omen.

"I'm a fool," I say. "I saw her die." But I imagine a last-minute panic, Ashley leaving to find her mother on the other side of the city while I stayed behind, and that scenario suddenly seems just as likely. I remember none of it... but it has the power of possibility. "A damn fool."

I walk toward the house. It looks just as overgrown and abandoned as all the others. Of course it does; if she was still here, she wouldn't want to advertise the fact. Maybe there are many people still at home... letting the grass grow, the plants make a tangle of their garden... awaiting someone like me to come and rescue them from the certainty of their deaths.

The front door is closed, as I had left it. Empty milk bottles stand in their wire cage, awaiting collection. I shade the glass in the door and press my face to it. Inside seems quiet, undisturbed, and wholly alien to me.

I knock, smile, shake my head, and force the door open with three hefty kicks. It rebounds from the hall wall and I hold it open. The house is silent. "It's me," I say. There's no answer.

I don't know this place. There are pictures on the wall that I remember buying, but they're strange to me now.

The painted hall wall had taken me two whole weekends to finish, but it's as if this is the first time I've seen it. The air of the house, the space, is all wrong, and I cannot find it in myself to know it as home.

I step over the threshold and head for the stairs. I have no desire to see the rest of the house, because there's nothing here for me. Only the bedroom. That's where I remember leaving Ashley's corpse because I could not face burying her. So if my memory is not lying, if I'm not quite as mad as I think, if she really is dead... that's where she will be.

I climb thirteen stairs and stop on the landing. There's a smell. It's not rot or decay, isn't even that unpleasant. Maybe it's just the aroma of a house that has been locked up for six months with no ventilation. Even a home has to breathe.

Kidding myself, I think. *That's Ashley I smell, or what's left of her. Do I really need to see?*

And of course, I do.

I walk forward, pass the bathroom door, the spare bedroom, and stand before our bedroom door. Suddenly there is a rush of memory, so intense and raw that I sway and hold onto the banister to prevent myself from falling. A scratch on the door from when we moved in our new bed. A pluck at the corner of the landing carpet where I hadn't fitted it quite right, and the vacuum cleaner kept snagging it. A splash of paint on the skirting to the right of the door, from when I was decorating the walls; I'd always intended cleaning it off. Every memory involved Ashley's presence, but none of them involved *her*, as a visible, touchable entity. Still she is so far away from me, and on the other side of a door.

"Well, standing here won't solve anything," I say. "Ash, I'm coming in."

I push open the door. And there she is.

A few minutes later, sitting in the street beyond my front garden, wallowing in memories of Ashley that are all mine, I see the first of the shapes milling at the entrance to the cul-de-sac. I think it's Cordell and I stand to wave, but then other shapes join the first, moving cautiously or awkwardly into the street, and I know that I'm in trouble.

So here they are. The zombie hordes, the survivors turned to cannibalism, the gang ruled by a sadistic ex-military man intent on gaining control of the nothing that's left. Here is the Armageddon I imagined as a child. And for a moment, content in remembering Ashley without having to drink to see her beautiful face once again, I really don't care.

SEVEN

HOLY GRAIL ALE

Ashley was crying again, her hair catching the glow of sunlight through the open window blinds, and this would be one of the days of my life. I went to her and held her as I always did at times like this. And as always, there was nothing I could say.

Later, we drove out into the country to one of our favourite pubs. We listened to Thin Lizzy on the stereo, their classic *Live and Dangerous* album, and we were both silent as Lynott gave his perfect rendition of "Still in Love with You." Our windows were down, our spirits rising, and Ashley rested her hand on my thigh as I drove. I touched the back of her hand now and then, but the country lanes were narrow and twisty, and I spent a lot of time changing gears.

When we reached the pub and parked, Ashley turned to me and said, "Everything's going to be all right." She smiled. And even though her eyes were still rimmed red from crying, I believed her.

It was cool, but we kept our jackets on and sat outside, listening to the tinkle of their old water feature. There was a main road half a mile away and the background hum of traffic was constant, but it still felt quite peaceful here. It was early evening, so there weren't many customers yet. We had a corner of the garden to ourselves.

Ashley went in to buy a drink, and she came out with two bottles of Black Sheep Monty Python's Holy Grail Ale and pint glasses. I smiled, but my stomach fell. A novelty beer such as this surely couldn't taste very good.

I was wrong. It was a nice pint—pale amber, light and fruity, subtly bitter and dusty at the end—and the bottle labels gave us a laugh.

Ashley sat beside me, eschewing eye contact for the sake of closeness.

"So what are we going to do?" she asked.

"Sit here and drink some more."

She nudged me. "We have yet to toss a coin to see who's driving home."

I shrugged, looked around, let the setting sun warm my face. "Fuck it," I said. "Let's stay here and call a cab later."

"Sounds good," she said, but she drifted off and became contemplative. Ran her finger around the rim of her glass. I knew she had meant something different. "So," she said after a minute or two, "what are we going to do?"

I stroked her back. "What do you want to do?"

"We could adopt," she said.

"Really?"

"I don't know."

I took a drink and sighed. "Well, it's something to think about."

Ashley and I were very good at talking. We knew each other so well, knew how to pitch a conversation, when to start or when to stop. That evening we spent chatting about many inconsequentialities, the sort of things couples often talk about when they spend time relaxed together. Music, films, sex, food, sex, and sex. But all the while, interspersed through our casual conversation like a lifeline through an avalanche of experience, we kept coming back to the subject at hand: Ashley could not have children, and we were faced with the first real challenge of our relationship.

"I want to do you from behind later," I said.

"If you're lucky."

"If *you're* lucky."

She laughed and took a drink. "Long as you let me sit on your face first."

"Hmmm… that's a tough one."

She laughed again, finished her drink, tapped the glass along the tabletop and listened to the different notes it made. "Imagine a future without anything of us in it," she said. "No genes of ours. Not even any ideas. No one who'll lie awake at night and think about us, about all the good times we gave them through their childhood."

"We adopt, it still won't be our genes," I said. "It never can be."

Ashley tapped the glass harder. "Well, that's not what's important. It's memory that's important. If no one carries our memory when we die, then we really are dead."

I thought about that for a while, and I didn't like what

she said. I saw the stark truth of it. No children, no fond memories of us as kind parents or doting grandparents. Our friends would remember us until they died, and perhaps their children would occasionally talk of the nice couple their mum and dad used to spend time with, nice but a little sad too. Because we would become sad, I knew. However much we loved each other and supported each other through this, we would become sad.

"So we adopt," I said.

"It's not that easy."

"There are agencies, people who help."

She looked at me and smiled, leant forward and kissed me full on the lips. "I don't mean that," she said.

I went to get more drinks, and when I came back Ashley was knelt down beside the pub's garden pond. I could see a swathe of her bare back, and the top of her thong peeked above her shorts. I handed her a glass and squatted behind her, nudging against her so she could feel how turned on I was. "Definitely from behind," I whispered, aware now that the garden was filling with patrons.

"If you're lucky," she said.

"If *you're* lucky."

We drank some more, ate a small bar snack, called a cab and went home. We were drunk, and we became quite heated in the back of the taxi. No kissing or ripping of clothes, but my hand rested at the top of her thigh, my little finger massaging between her legs and feeling the heat of her there. And half a mile from home she casually unzipped my jeans and let my erection spring free. I had to continue responding to the driver's banter as she stroked me, and when we stopped I somehow managed to get to our front door without being seen.

It was one of those days I remembered forever. But we never had children, and we never did adopt, and now so many memories are mine and mine alone.

I sit astride the bike, kick it to life and watch the shapes coming closer. There are a dozen of them. They're people, faces blank, dirty, shorn of civilisation. Their clothes are old but not too ragged, and each of them carries a strange weapon. I see no guns, but there are sharpened bed posts, umbrellas spiked with nails, a child's plastic doll embedded with rusty razor blades. It's as if these people are hefting the dead past as a weapon.

I'm unsettled, nervous, but not scared. Ashley is with me now, and she always will be. Those remains up in the bedroom are not her. By coming here I have lifted her memory away from that room of death and placed it firmly in my mind, unlocking a million doorways and leaving them ready to be opened. Whether I do that whilst alive or dead does not matter.

I rev the bike and the shapes pause. They exchange glances, but nothing seems to pass between them. And in that moment my fear breaks through, and I begin to make out more details.

The shapes are wearing more than clothes. One of them has a necklace of yellowed bones. Another seems to have a face covered in sharp white spots, and they could be embedded teeth. One girl—she can't be more than thirteen—has a skull protruding above her head, tied on with a couple of leather belts. The skull has a smashed jaw and several obvious fractures. The girl does not smile or frown. She is as expressionless as her gruesome decoration.

There's more, but I don't want to see. I rev the bike again and try to judge whether I can make it past them. They're spread out across the road, advancing in a clumsy, slow line, and I suppose I could ride straight through them. But even though they appear slow and apathetic now, they still have weapons. I imagine the blade-strewn doll being thrown at my face when I'm going twenty miles per hour.

Something draws my attention upward, and a shadow slips across the sky. It glides, swoops, flits from here to there without really making itself known. I squint against the bright sky but that does not make seeing it any easier. *Just like back in the city near the Manor. Seen from a distance, those flying things we were content to leave alone.* It's closer now, and though I still can't make it out—or perhaps I'm too scared to admit what it is—I'm now in its domain.

And then there's a noise from farther away, louder and more violent than the deathly shuffles of these lost people. A gunshot, the scream of an engine struggling to overcome some obstacle, a shout. I turn my head slightly so that I can hear more, and the shapes before me screech.

They run at me. All pretence at lethargy now broken, I'm more shocked than I should be. I kick the bike into gear but my foot slips on the clutch, I tip sideways, and my knee takes all the weight as I lever myself upright again, twisting the throttle, leaving a line of hot rubber on the ground behind me, aiming across the street at the timber front gate of the Barkers' garden. My only advantage now is that I know the lie of the land here, and in those shapes' once-blank faces I haven't seen anyone I recognise.

Once-blank, because now they're twisted into expressions of pure hunger, and hate.

I stand slightly as the bike bumps over the low kerb. The Barkers' gate smashes open, hinges squealing. A woman tries to grab me as I enter the front garden. Her fingers curl through a cloth loop on my jacket's shoulder and I throw all my weight forward, changing into second gear and hauling on the throttle. For a moment I think I'm going to be pulled backward from the bike—I'm sure the woman is actually being dragged along behind me—then she screams and falls free.

I glance back to see the others trampling over the woman as they pursue me. She's shouting something that sounds like, "Davey! Davey!"

I steer beside the house, slowing slightly so that I can step the bike along the narrow path between the garage and boundary hedge. The hedge has blossomed and expanded, and I have to use the bike's power to pull me past the grasping, tangled branches. The people are close again as I burst into the Barkers' back garden, and I give them a face full of exhaust fumes as I power the bike at the back gate. This one is also made of wood but it's stronger, the locks better maintained, and at the last second I realise my mistake. I lean back, the bike's front wheel strikes the gate, and I'm thrown forward and up as the bike rises onto its front wheel.

I end up sprawled on the ground at the base of the fence, motorbike idling on its side beside me, and by some miracle I haven't been crushed. I shake my head, dizzied by an impact I can't even remember.

Another flying thing passes directly over the garden, too fast to see. It leaves a hint of jasmine on the air, and below that a smell I don't want to recognise.

There's a triumphant whoop and the people run at me. "Eating tonight!" one of them screeches. It could even be the young girl. Her eyes are wide, the injured skull waving wildly above her head as she runs.

There's a roar behind the fence, the explosion of a car horn being leant on, and the people pause, staring up over my head.

A shotgun fires. The woman with the teeth embedded in her face crumples, her mouth a circle of shock as the front of her dress turns wet. Her hands go to the wound, and inside.

The gate is kicked open and there is Cordell, hauling at my arms, shouting at me to stand. I see panic on his face, and fear, and anger as well, because I've dragged them into this situation and as far as he's concerned there was no need.

"Come on, come on!"

"The bike," I say.

"Fuck the bike!"

"I'm taking it."

"Leave the bike," a gruff voice says, and one of the men takes a quick run toward us. The shotgun roars again and his shoulder explodes. He goes down, arm flapping.

"I'm taking the bike," I say to Cordell. I'm standing, my

legs and arms work, and that's good enough for me.

"Fuck's sake," he says quietly, and I can see all the anger now. He glances up at the sky, down again. "Your choice. Follow us, then. It's not pretty out there, and we won't stop for you on the way out."

"Thanks for coming," I say.

Cordell giggles, a frightening sound. "Thanks for the invite!" He giggles again, then helps me lift the bike.

The people are standing in a line from the side of the Barkers' house to where the man with the shattered shoulder writhes on the ground. They're not looking at us anymore. They're looking at the man, and the woman with the wound in her stomach. Staring at them. Their faces are not quite as blank as before they had charged me, though the violence seems to have gone from them. I see hunger.

Cordell is right, it's not pretty out there. I ride between the Range Rovers, so I don't see everything that goes on. But the shotgun fires several more times, I hear the impact of bodies against metal, and three times I have to veer quickly as a crushed body appears from beneath the vehicle ahead of me. Once I ride straight over a man, unable to avoid him without crashing the bike into a lamp post. He screams as I wheel across his already crushed stomach. I even say sorry.

Looking to the left and right I can see people standing along the side of the street. Not many of them—maybe a dozen between my cul-de-sac and where the houses stop before the motorway—but they all look similar to those that had attacked me. Still human, but only just.

Desperate. Hungry.

I know what they were after, but I can barely acknowledge it, not right now. It'll take time to sink in. If these *are* the things Billy and Lucy have locked in that ambulance, what do they intend doing with them?

More shapes flit by above us. None of them come any lower, none attack. I'm being to wonder whether they're really there.

With violence and screaming we leave Newport behind, drive onto the motorway and make our way as far from there as we can. I'm cold, even though the sun is still warming my skin. I've been stupid. But everywhere I look, every scene I take in, is tinged now with a memory of Ashley. After six months I feel the grief beginning to hit home. I can't help smiling.

"Fucking idiot!" the Irishman says. He doesn't shout and rage, and in a way that's worse. This is a very controlled anger.

"I'm sorry," I say. "I had to go, to see."

"Because of what that nut case said?"

"No, not really because of that at all."

We are milling around the vehicles while Cordell and Jessica change a flat tyre on the lead Range Rover. The old tyre has several nails embedded in it, probably picked up in the city. Something else I feel responsible for.

"Don't pick on him," Jacqueline says. "This is strange for all of us."

"Strange? Did you see those people back there? What they wore, what they carried?"

"They haven't moved on like we have," I say. "Michael said they'd be out here."

"Yes, but he didn't suggest we go *looking* for them."

"I'm sorry," I say again. I've already thanked them all for coming after me, and I don't want to lessen my gratitude by belabouring it.

The Irishman shakes his head, runs his fingers through his hair. "So, find what you went looking for?"

"Yes," I say.

"Good." He walks away, and I can tell that his anger is already abating.

"Fixed," Cordell says. "Let's go. We can make another few miles before sunset. Then I think we should camp. What do you all think?"

"Good idea," Jacqueline says. She glances at me and smiles, and I mount the motorbike.

We're riding away from the setting sun, and it throws my long, reaching shadow before me.

Later, parked beside the toll booths before the Severn Bridge, we all sit in one of the Range Rovers to eat. Conversation returns to Billy and Lucy, and Cordell mentions that he caught a glimpse inside their metal container. "Like an armoury in there," he says. "Guns and boxes of stuff everywhere."

"It's what was in the ambulance that interests me," Jessica says.

Jacqueline shakes her head. "Not me. Don't want to know. Not me."

"I wonder what they're *really* doing there," I say.

"Waiting for someone," Cordell says.

The Irishman snorts. "Strange place to wait."

"Close to the city, so they can drive in quickly," I muse. "Close to the motorway for a quick escape."

Cordell nods. "And enough weapons to fight a small war."

"Wonder where they found them," Jessica says.

We drift into silence, eat, sharing an occasional nervous glance. But most of the time we look outside.

During the hour it took us to drive from Newport to where we are camped, we saw wolves on the hillsides, something larger—a bear, the Irishman said—splashing in an irrigation ditch, and a minibus stalled in the middle of the road with blood and bones decorating its insides. No disease deaths there. Cordell swears he saw teeth and claw marks on some of the bones when he went to investigate. The rest of us stayed away.

"Well, we're moving on," Jessica says, breaking the silence with a sigh.

"Aren't we just." I think of the things Michael said, and I too wonder at the true identity of those things inside the ambulance. More of the mad, hungry people from the city, or something else?

And were there more of them on the prowl?

We cross the Severn Bridge and drive another fifteen miles that evening. The light is good and the sky is clear, so we decide that it would be wiser to move while we can. "The sooner we get to Bar None, the better," the Irishman says. As I'm riding the bike—battered from its two recent spills, but still functioning perfectly well—I wonder whether that's the case at all.

None of us really know what we'll find when we get there.

We stop eventually on the hard shoulder, camouflaging the vehicles between a succession of broken-down and burnt-out lorries. Cordell finds an empty cattle truck and we agree that, with its viewing slots, it's an ideal place to camp.

So begins our first night away from the mansion in six months.

As the sun goes down, the first strange sounds rise.

Since my teens, I've loved listening to the countryside at night. There are very few areas where you can still really do that without the background hum of civilisation intruding. There's always a distant road that carries cars and lorries late into the night, a train track that supports midnight transports between factories and foundries, or the noises of a town asleep. A sleeping town is like a sleeping person; it rumbles and clicks, snores and groans. Electric lines hum. Cats howl, fight and rut. Vehicles tick as they cool down, and there's always a TV or radio keeping some insomniac or night-shift worker company while their family sleeps nearby.

It's very, very rare to hear nature at its rawest. I used to think I could. I occasionally drove out into the country at night, sometimes with Ashley, more often on my own, and I thought I'd found a few places where wilderness still survived. Places where the touch of humanity had yet to reach: on top of a hillside, past the end of a track in the local forest, deep in one of the valleys of mid-Wales. I sat away from my car, stared at a sky unpolluted by artificial light, and listened. And I thought I heard a nature that was, for a time, ignorant of humanity.

Sitting in the cattle truck beside civilisation's clogged tarmac artery, I realise how wrong I was. *This* is nature. *This* is the natural order of things, without the influence of humanity to weigh things down or scare them into silence. Perhaps some of the creatures we hear outside were born into a world without people, offspring of animals that lived through the plagues and celebrated by giving birth to their first truly free descendants. Perhaps many of them are older that that, but in the six months since the end of humanity's reign on the planet they have forgotten how things used to be. Whatever the case, the night is filled with howls, growls and cries of freedom; things hunting and mating, stalking and eating.

"They've forgotten we're here," Jessica says.

"Good," says Jacqueline.

"I recognise some of them," the Irishman says. "But not all."

"Fox," I say, and it sounds like a screaming baby.

"Badger."

A creature coughs and barks nearby, perhaps as close as the ditch bordering the adjacent field. "Dog?" Jessica asks.

"Maybe." I shrug. "There must be thousands gone feral."

"Always had it in them," the Irishman says. "Never trusted a fucking canine in my life. They fooled us with their puppy-dog eyes, their begging, their rolling over to play dead. All they ever wanted was our meat." He grins at me and starts to snicker.

"You're a bad movie trailer," I say, and the two of us

laugh. Nobody else seems amused, because that really doesn't sound like any dog we've heard before. It's a bark that says something, rather than just a shout to get our attention.

"*Do* you think they know we're here?" Jacqueline says. She stands at the edge of the cattle truck and looks out through one of the slits. I used to hate these vehicles when I was a kid, seeing all those sheep or cows crammed in on their way to be slaughtered or sold. They always looked so helpless in there, the lucky ones able to stick their noses out through the slits to catch one final breath of freedom before their skulls were holed.

"I'm sure they do," Jessica says. "They'll smell us."

Jacqueline looks for a full minute before sitting with us again. She hugs her jacket tight around her shoulders and crossed arms. "I can't see anything."

Something lands on the roof of the truck and scampers across the metal, the sound ending as the creature leaps and lands on the soft grass verge with a low thump. It snickers and runs away.

"I need a drink," I say. The others nod and agree in hushed tones, and Jessica and the Irishman open two bottles of wine. Cordell hands out some plastic cups and we each have a cupful of good Merlot. I drain mine quickly. Never was one to sip wine and appreciate its delicate aroma, dance of flavours, full body. Sometimes, I just want to get drunk.

"I've got a couple of beers in my bag," the Irishman says. He smiles at me, nods, and hands me a bottle. "Knew you'd appreciate that." It's Summer Lightning, rich and full of the taste of sunshine.

"Thanks," I say. "You're sure?"

"Wine's good for me," the Irishman says, and the others nod and agree.

Damn, I wish I knew his name! I smile and take the bottle opener from my pocket. Church key, a friend once called it. Allowing entrance to wonders. In this darkened cattle truck, with the sounds of nature known and mysterious deepening the darkness around us, the snick of the lid flipping from the bottleneck makes me feel at home.

"We're so alone," Jacqueline says. "So forgotten."

"We've got hope, now," Jessica replies, and I wonder once again what she lost.

Jacqueline shrugs and drains her wine. "I don't know. Maybe we were clutching at straws."

"What do you mean?" Cordell asks.

"None of us know who he was. Where he came from. Where he went."

"He was here to help us."

"Was he?" Jacqueline pours more wine, stands and stares from the slits in the side of the truck again. "Still nothing out there."

The dark sings with nighttime things, proving Jacqueline wrong.

We take turns, four of us sleeping while the fifth holds the shotgun and keeps a watch, and a listen. I don't think I am sleeping well, but when Cordell wakes me with a harsh nudge, it takes a few seconds for things to arrange themselves in my head. *Nobody to remember me*, I think, and then I see the look on Cordell's face.

"Jacqueline's dead," he says. "I was keeping watch, and she was sleeping so deeply I decided to take her watch too, and—"

"Hush it!" the Irishman says. "Even if you hadn't fallen asleep, you wouldn't have saved her."

"How can you know that?"

I'm confused. *Dead?*

Jessica stands from the body in the corner. "She died in her sleep, Cordell. I don't know why… maybe her heart just stopped. But look at her." She steps back, inviting us all to look at the body.

"Is that really Jacqueline?" I ask. It's a stupid thing to say, but no one comments. Maybe for a moment they all think the same thing.

"She looks so peaceful," the Irishman says.

"She doesn't look like herself," I say. "So calm."

"Maybe that's how she was before the plagues," Cordell whispers. "And now she's back to how she should be."

We all stand quietly for a while, looking at the huddled form of Jacqueline in the corner of the cattle truck, trying to accept what has happened. In a world where billions have died, this one extra death is so difficult to understand.

"I'll check," Jessica says, her voice fragile as glass, and we all know what she means. She's going to strip Jacqueline and search for signs of disease. What good it will do… If she has died from one of the rampant plagues that brought on the end, there's nothing any of us can do about it. We have no idea how we survived; we have no idea why Jacqueline died.

"Maybe she just gave in," I say as I jump from the truck. Cordell follows, standing quietly by my side. I nudge his arm. "Hey. She just gave in."

"You can't know that," he says. "I took her turn at watch. If I'd woken her like I was supposed to—"

"Then she'd have died tomorrow instead of tonight."

He stares at me, and for a moment I see something troubling in his eyes. Anger? Hatred? I'm not sure, but I don't like it. "At least it would have been one more day," he says quietly. "I need a piss." He walks into the ditch beside the motorway and faces away from me, into the field.

The Irishman climbs from the truck, holding his back and groaning as he stretches. He looks at the sky and lights a cigarette. "Gonna be a nice day," he says.

"Really."

"Hey." He touches my face, a shockingly familiar gesture that brings a lump to my throat. "She's no better or worse off than us, you know? It's all borrowed time now."

"We'll remember her," I say.

He frowns, nods. "'Course we will. And when we get to Bar None, we'll raise a few for Jacqueline."

Cordell finishes urinating and climbs the fence into the neighbouring field. There will be no crops this year, but the field is alive with grasses and plants of many varieties. I can hear the hush of stalks against his jeans. A few butterflies rise and flutter away from him, and a cloud of flies forms around his head. He waves at them absently, and I can hear him sobbing.

"He blames himself," I say.

"Nah." Sometimes the Irishman tells me, with a smile bordering on hysteria, that cigarettes are bad for his health. This one he inhales deeply, closing his eyes and letting the smoke drift from his mouth as if testing the breeze.

"You think not?"

The Irishman shakes his head. "Just that there's one less of us now."

I go to say more, but then Jessica jumps from the rear of the cattle truck. She lands awkwardly. She's crying, and that comes as a shock.

"I don't know how she died," she says.

"Just gave up," the Irishman says, and he steps carefully into the ditch and up the other side. He enters the field and walks slowly after Cordell, cigarette smoke hanging in the air to mark his route.

Jessica comes to me and I see her need, lifting my arm and letting her hang onto me for a while. I suspect I'm hanging onto her as well. Her tears are sharp and dry, bitter, and she soon brings herself under control. I don't know what to say.

"Lost someone," she says at last. I'm surprised, thinking that she's opening up, spilling her contained grief.

"Who?"

"Jacqueline. I lost her. No one else, and I feel so selfish crying over that. You—*everyone*—you've all lost so much more."

I think of Ashley, but I try not to make this about me.

Jessica rubs at her face, smearing an errant tear across her cheek. "It's hard," she says. "Poor Jacqueline." She sighs and moves away from me, creating her own space again. Already she seems back to her normal self.

"We should bury her," I say. For some reason, I think

an important moment has passed us by, untouched and unnoticed.

"In the ditch." Jessica points down at the trickle of water standing in the drainage channel.

"The ditch?"

"It's a better burial than most. And it'll be easier to dig. We don't have the right tools."

I begin digging the grave in the side of the ditch. There's a garden hoe in one of the Range rovers, and in the driver's cab of the cattle truck we find an old leather bag containing rusted builder's tools; a trowel, a plane, a hammer. I loosen the soil with the hoe to begin with, them scoop it up and out with the trowel. It's wet but not soaked, and though the muck is heavy, it means that the hole's sides don't collapse.

I work up a sweat and it feels good. For a while I forget why I'm digging this hole. Every now and then the reason smashes back at me, and I remember Jacqueline whispering in the dark corners of the mansion while the rest of us debated, argued and laughed. She never really did any of that. She offered opinions, sometimes, but they were usually disguised as fears. That's the way she'd been living her life, day by day since the end: afraid.

But when I can forget the reason for the hole, I enjoy the physical exercise. After half an hour the Irishman and Cordell return, and Cordell insists on taking his turn. I'm happy to hand over the hoe and trowel. We all stay close as he digs. I don't know what the Irishman has said to him, but there's something dark gone from his face. He doesn't smile—I don't think I ever see him smile again—but he no longer looks alone.

Jessica takes a turn, and then the Irishman jumps into the rough hole and hacks at the ground with the hoe. He pulls out several great chunks of concrete left over from the road construction, and then climbs out.

"Deep enough," Cordell says. "I'll get her." He climbs into the back of the truck and the three of us wait there awkwardly, listening to the truck's suspension creaking, not looking at each other. He appears at the gate with Jacqueline held in both arms. Suddenly, she looks dead. In the truck she may have been enjoying a peaceful asleep, but now her head's hanging back, her long hair trailing on the ground, and her arms sway with every slight movement.

I go to help but Cordell shakes his head. He steps carefully down the side of the wide ditch, reaches the hole and lowers Jacqueline in. Her feet touch first and he nearly drops her, but he manages to catch her by the arms and lower her down. He brushes a few errant strands of hair from her face, lays her arms alongside her body, and climbs from the hole.

The four of us stand there, looking down at our dead friend and wondering what to say. She's already moved on from this world, and to me the dark sides of the hole look like the beginning of another.

"Did anyone know a song she liked?" Cordell asks.

No one speaks.

"A poem? A book?"

More silence. And after a while, Cordell asks the question that makes us realise just how little we knew Jacqueline. "Does anyone know what religion she is?"

So we stand there for a while saying nothing, because

none of us can think of anything to say. I'm glad nobody offers up a prayer. It's been a long time since I've spoken to God, and I can't see that He'd have any place here right now.

My stomach rumbles. The Irishman glances at me, eyes glittering.

"We should head off," Cordell says. "Long way to go."

It only takes us a few minutes to cover Jacqueline with the wet soil. We leave her face until last, as if hoping it was all a mistake and she will splutter herself awake. But her eyes remain closed, even as earth patters down on them, and we hide her pale skin from whatever the world has become.

We decide to continue with both Range Rovers and the bike. The bike is my idea; I love riding it, having time to think my own thoughts without feeling responsible for someone else. Cordell drives one vehicle, saying he'd prefer to be alone. Jessica drives the other with the Irishman for company.

"We make good time, we may even get there today," Jessica says.

"Hope so." I'm pulling on the heavy jacket. It's already warm, but I've come off the bike twice so far. Third time, maybe I won't be so lucky. I'll take a bit of sweat and discomfort in exchange for some decent padding. If only we had a helmet.

"Think we should mark it?" the Irishman says. He's looking back at Jacqueline's grave.

"No," Cordell says. "Let's leave her alone."

"It's quiet," I say, and for the first time I really notice

just how quiet it's become. No birds singing in the trees, no animals calling from across the fields. Not even a breeze to carry our voices away.

"They see and hear us now," the Irishman says.

We break the silence with our engines and go on our way.

The road is surprisingly clear. We pass many cars, lorries, vans, buses, crashed motorcycles, and even a couple of tractors, but it's rare we have to stop and push vehicles out of the way. There are frequent pile-ups, and occasionally the twisted wreckage is burnt black, road melted and reset around the chaos. At one point we pass an accident on the other carriageway involving at least a hundred vehicles, swathes of them distorted and charred by terrible fires. The central barrier is bent and buckled with the weight of the calamity, but it succeeded in letting nothing through. It must have been awful. I cruise by slowly, and as we round a slow bend and head up a hillside I can see how far back the waiting traffic is piled. It's nose to bumper, side to side, all three lanes of the motorway and the hard shoulder jammed with vehicles. I can see the noses and tails of cars and trucks protruding from the ditch on the far side, and I wonder how many of them had been forced off the road.

There are bodies, of course. Hundreds of them, thousands. I don't see many, because all the car windows are up and most of them are slick with moss and rot. I pass by so much tragedy and try to imagine none of it, though I'm not totally successful. I see one car with a burst suitcase strapped to its roof, clothes and fluffy toys leaking out, and I cannot help but imagine the scene inside as the parents and children died.

It's horrible. Unbearable. I begin to cry, but it's anger I feel most of all. If only I had something or someone at whom to direct that anger. A reason, a cause, an explanation for all of this. But life is a mystery now more than ever before. Death can never offer an easy answer.

We travel for three hours before stopping for food and a drink. Jessica passes around some water, but then the Irishman opens a bottle of wine and we all gratefully accept a plastic cup. It's white and warm and I crave a beer, but it still tastes good.

The sun is bright and hot today, sky devoid of clouds. We sit behind the Range Rovers beside the road, and if I look directly out across the fields I cannot see any wrecked cars. It's almost as if nothing has happened. The countryside is wilder than usual, and the fields no longer have their regimented look, but if I close my eyes I can almost believe we're back in normal times.

If only I could hear an aircraft passing overhead, or the baying of cows, or the slow drone of para-gliders taking off from the neighbouring hills.

At some point I drift into sleep, and I begin to remember for real.

EIGHT

SUMMER LIGHTNING

It took me a long time to find the house I really wanted. Six months to sell my London flat, another three months living in rented accommodation in Cardiff, but then I travelled to West Wales for a weekend and I found this house, and we fell in love with each other.

Sounds strange, a house falling in love with a person. But that's what happened. When I arrived to view, the front door was unlocked, even though the estate agent said no one had been inside for almost six weeks. I opened the door and entered, and I knew where everything was. I had never been here before—never even been to West Wales—but to the left was the kitchen, down the hallway and under the stairs was the door to the study, to the right was the living room, and if I walked through there and opened the double doors I'd see the dining room, painted white and dominated by an old oak dining suite rescued from a dilapidated manor house years earlier.

I *knew*. But I went through the motions anyway, mainly because I was *scared* that I knew. Perhaps I wanted to find something I did not recognise, a room I had never imagined which would make my recollection of somewhere I had never been imperfect. And that imperfection would bring comfort. So I looked downstairs and up, and found nothing out of place.

By the time I opened the back door and went into the garden, I knew that I loved the house. There was no fear or confusion, just a certainty that I should be here, and I sat on a flaking metal chair on the timber decking and rang the estate agent. He called back five minutes later to accept my offer. Four weeks later, I was in.

The sun was kissing the horizon. The wine sat in a cooler before me, resting on the metal table I had bought to match the garden furniture already there. I sat on the same metal chair; repainted now, and softened by a thick cushion. I closed my eyes and sighed.

"It's a beautiful night," I said.

I opened my eyes when somebody screamed.

The voice had come from the other side of the house. I dropped my wine glass, jumped aside as it shattered on the decking and ran indoors. Cool shadows welcomed me in and eased me back out, and I ran down the short gravelled driveway to the quiet country road beyond.

There was another scream just before I reached the front gates, coming from behind the screen of leylandii bordering my property. This scream was more controlled and considered, and more filled with panic.

I opened the smaller of the two gates, stepped out into the road and saw the girl in white. She must have been sixteen or seventeen, certainly no older, and her dazzling trousers and blouse were spattered with blood. She had fallen from her bike. She held her hand up in front of her, staring at the intermittent spray of blood showering from her wrist.

"Oh, Jesus Christ!" I said.

The girl looked at me, wide white eyes in a blood-mask.

As I ran to her I slipped the belt from my jeans and the phone from my pocket. I dialled emergency, knelt beside the girl and smiled as I waited for the connection. I switched the phone to loudspeaker and sat it beside me on the road.

As I spoke to the dispatcher, told her where we were and what had happened, I tied the belt around the girl's arm. Pulled tight. Slipped the clasp together and raised her hand higher.

I had no idea what I was doing.

The dispatcher insisted on remaining on the line, but it was the girl I spoke to.

"What's your name?"

"Jemma."

"What happened?"

"I fell off my bike."

I almost laughed. Stupid question, obvious answer.

Jemma's panic had lessened now that I had taken control. Blood still ran from the gash on her wrist and palm, but it no longer sprayed, so I hoped that was good.

"Is she woozy?" the telephone said.

Jemma shook her head and I said no.

"You live there?" she said, nodding back at the house.

"Yes. Not long."

"It's a lovely place," she said. "I was in there once, when the last owners were there. Couple of years ago. It felt like home." She looked away, embarrassed, but I nodded and told her I knew what she meant.

I asked Jemma if she wanted to come inside but the dispatcher told us to wait by the roadside, because the ambulance was on its way. So we sat in the sun, and I loosened the belt every few minutes to allow some blood through, and it was as though we'd known each other for ages. Jemma was no longer scared, and adrenaline kept me going.

It was later, when they'd taken her away and said she'd be fine, and the house had welcomed me back inside—my new house, my home—that I started to shake, spilling tears and gasping for air as massive sobs shook me to the floor.

I wake, sit up, crying. The Irishman is sitting with his back to me, and he doesn't turn around. I silently curse his politeness.

"Holy shit," I say.

"What?" Cordell is behind me, and I stand and turn around.

The house... that voice... my home?

I shake my head. "Bad dream." I look around, searching for a sign that there were reasons for that memory, but I find none.

"We should go," Jessica says. "You okay?"

I nod, run my hands across my scalp. *Damn! That was weird. That was...*

I mount the bike, kick it to life and fill my head with noise before I allow myself to admit what has happened.

That was Jacqueline. I had one of her memories.

A dozen miles later, travelling toward the falling sun, we see something that stops us in our tracks: a forest, starting immediately beside the motorway and spread up and across the low hills of Somerset. It sweeps away from the road, climbing slopes, spiking hilltops, and looking along the road's route I cannot see where the trees end. They look young and fresh—their leaves sporting vivid shades of green, visible trunks quite smooth and unworn by time—and I wonder how long they have taken to grow.

The others climb from the Range Rovers, I dismount, and we stand together beside the road.

"That doesn't look quite right," Cordell says.

I laugh, but it's a desperate sound. "I drove this way several times each year," I say. "This shouldn't be here. There should be farms out there, and a hotel up on that hill with panoramic glass windows, and barns and a field full of junked cars half a mile that way." I point at the trees, the trees. There's no sign of any buildings, anywhere. No power pylons, no flashes of tumbled masonry, and no fields outlined by wild hedges or old stone walls. Only trees, with dozens of birds spotting the sky above. We can see quite a long way into the forest, because the leaves seem not to have grown into a full canopy yet. But that's the only real sign that these trees have not been here for very long.

How long ago? I think. *How long since Ashley and I came*

down here? I'm not sure what to feel. I suppose I should be scared. We're standing before something supernatural, after all: a forest that was not here a year before. Yet so much has happened that the term *natural* has taken on new meaning, and continues to change.

"We'll go in," the Irishman says. His voice is lacking in his usual lightness. "There'll be plenty to see in there." He starts across the hard shoulder toward the overgrown hedge that marks the edge of relative normality.

"Hey," I say. "It may not be safe."

The Irishman turns and shrugs. "What is?"

The trees whisper.

I take a step back and almost trip. Jessica gasps and reaches for the shotgun. There was not even a breeze, and only a few leaves seem to flicker and shift.

The Irishman pauses before the hedge and stands on tiptoes to see over. He looks left and right, stumbling a couple of times as he tries to stretch higher. When he drops down onto flat feet he seems smaller than before. Shrunken.

"What is it?" I say.

"Dangerous in there," he says. He joins us back on the road and looks left and right, examining the motionless queue of vehicles. "Notice anything?"

We look, and yes, I have already noticed. Perhaps it just didn't register before.

"Doors are open," Jessica says. "We've seen a few before, but there are lots more here. As if there was something to stop and get out for."

"They're in there." The Irishman nods at the forest, then turns and climbs back into his Range Rover. He shuts the door, and the sun glares from glass so that I only see him in silhouette. Even then I know that he is shaking.

"Do you really want to see?" Jessica says. Cordell has started for the hedge, and even though I can answer Jessica's question I follow him. Some things need to be seen. The bodies in the cars can stay where they are, because they have chosen a very private death. The old cities clotted with dead and scattered with damaged survivors will never be somewhere for us, because they are so far in the past, awash with the stink of yesterday's rot and madness. But here, the supernatural gives us some way to glimpse something else. Something changed, perhaps, or of the future.

We reach the hedge together. I'm taller than the Irishman, and I can see more. Cordell finds a rusted paint pot hidden in the grass and stands on it. To begin with, we say nothing.

In this new forest, the trees are spaced far apart. The ground between them is rich with low plant life, some of it root crops gone wild, some wilder plants spread from the hedges or seeded by birds. There are none of the usual signs of an old, established wood: no fallen trunks, jagged stumps or banks of old shrubs. But there are people. I can see a dozen from where I stand, all of them involved somehow with the trunk of a tree. I can think of no other word that suits: they're *involved*.

A naked man is pressed against one trunk, the wood holding him tight where it has grown to encompass his abdomen and stomach, and even the tip of his nose and lips seem to be held still. He seems to be dead, though his pale skin is unmarked by decay. His hair is long and tangled, and I can see insects crawling in and out of its mess. There's a woman to my left, legs and arms protruding from either side of an oak tree's trunk. Her face is almost entirely out of sight, only a cheek, ear and length of golden hair still revealed. I can tell it's a woman because one breast is also loose, hanging as though heavy and full. There's an old man high in one tree's branches, pierced in several places and held aloft while leaves cloak him green. A child—I think it's a boy, though I cannot be sure—is buried to the chest in the junction at the top of an elm. The child's head hangs to the left, neck apparently broken. Still, no rot.

"They're alive," Cordell breathes.

"No. I don't think so."

"But their skin, their faces. They're still whole, and if they came from those cars…" He points back over one shoulder with his thumb, never taking his eyes from the trees.

"I think they're being kept," I say.

"Kept?" He glances at me then back at the trees, and I see realisation settling.

"What do you see?" Jessica calls.

"Dead people," I say.

Cordell shakes his head. "Kept for what?"

I have no idea, but he looks at me, demanding an answer. I shrug. "Food?"

"Food. But it's not *all* of them. Not *every* tree has someone."

"No. Maybe just the lucky ones."

There's another whisper from the trees, and I instinctively look up to see the patterns of leaves waving at the sky. But there is almost no movement. No breeze. The whisper goes on, and I know it has come from deep within this new forest.

I expect a head to turn then, a fist to clench, an exposed eye to blink slowly, a mouth to stretch into a smile, but none of that happens. The bodies remain still but whole, kept and protected from the ravages of decay by their new tree homes. I wonder whether they share more with the trees than just space.

"We need to go," Cordell says. He steps down from the paint pot and walks back to the road, and I can hear him mumble something to Jessica.

I take one last look, because it suddenly seems important to see. Nothing changes; there is no revelation. The trees whisper again as I turn to leave, but there is no calling in that sound, no lure. Perhaps it's a language we were never meant to know.

As I ride alone, I dwell upon the memory I had from Jacqueline's life. She must have told me about it during one of those long, sleepless nights when we lay together, for comfort and company rather than anything else. We had talked a lot then, drifting in and out of sleep, to and from dreams, and I revealed much more about myself in that bed than at any time since Ashley. Jacqueline did as well. I cannot recall the actual conversation when she talked about her new home in West Wales and the bloodied girl out on the road, but it must have happened. *Must* have.

But that felt like a memory of my own!

I ignore the voice of reason in my mind, because it's

surely mad.

That evening, as the sun finally sinks away, we park on the road and sit together in one vehicle. The sunset is giving us a wonderful display of colours as it settles low over the Devonshire hills. Cordell once said that the fine sunsets were caused by dust in the sky from a distant war. But he hadn't repeated that assumption for a while, and I was trying to forget.

"That's beautiful," the Irishman says.

"It is." I'm sitting behind him and I see the sunset through the frazzled ends of his long hair.

"We should be there tomorrow," Cordell says.

"You think so?" Jessica is in the driving seat. She's nursing the shotgun like a teddy bear.

"So long as the roads stay as clear as they have been, yes."

"What's happening?" she says. "What were those trees? Why were they holding dead people, like you said? What's happening?"

None of us answer for a while, and I feel the need to break the silence. "Michael told us things are moving on," I say.

"Great," the Irishman says. "Moving on to carnivorous fuckin' trees."

"They weren't eating them," Cordell says. "Not really."

"We stay to the road," I say. "We stick to the plan, get to Bar None as soon as we can."

"If it even exists." Cordell slips down in the seat beside me and looks at the Range Rover's ceiling. "Maybe Michael was a madman."

"You really believe that?" I ask. He closes his eyes.

"I have a plan," Jessica says. "If we don't find this place, I have a plan. There's a place on Bodmin, out on the moor, a hotel."

"Jamaica Inn," I say.

She smiles and nods. "We could go there. It's in the middle of nowhere, away from any towns or cities, and if there were people there at the end, I'll bet it wasn't many."

"Not many bodies to move, you mean," the Irishman says.

"Could be they're still alive."

"I'm not going out there," Cordell says. He nods at the windscreen but I know what he means, we all do. The wilds. "I'm staying on this road until we get to Bar None, then I'll go inside and see if what he said is true. And if it's all bollocks—if we don't even find the place—I'll turn around and drive all the way back home. I will. But there's no way you're dragging me onto the middle of Bodmin Moor. I've been there and it's *wild*. And that was before." He shakes his head. "No way."

"Well, it's just an idea."

"We've put so much trust in him," I say, and my words dwindle away into silence. We're all realising exactly what we've done: given up a safe place, come out into the changing world, opened ourselves up to danger, chasing the dream of a place that may or may not be, all on the strength of one man. Perhaps the end really has driven us mad.

We park the Range Rovers close together and sleep in

them. The Irishman and I chat for a while, but there's a weight of knowledge between us that makes idle conversation seem almost disrespectful. We've seen and sensed individual things that are strange and almost incomprehensible. Considered together, they give evidence of a huge change. I'm scared, and nervous, and thrilled.

"You know what I heard?" he says, breaking a loaded silence.

"I'm sure you'll tell me."

"Theories," he says. "The internet was alight with them in the weeks before the end. They appeared on all the usual conspiracy theory websites to begin with. I used to love all that bullshit: who shot Kennedy, how the moon landings were faked, who paid for Princess Diana to be assassinated. But pretty soon after they appeared on these sites, the major news agencies started to repeat the same stories. Details were slightly different, dates and places altered just subtly. But close enough."

"Is this the thing about the plagues' origins?"

"Yep. To begin with everyone thought it was just one plague out of Africa, like Ebola. But then it became clear that there were different strains, and from then on new plagues were identified every few days, and new points of origin were found. A cave in Indonesia. An inaccessible valley in Brazil. India, the Australian Outback, an ice-cave in Alaska discovered by oil drillers. Other places, too."

"Lots of people said it was terrorism."

"What terrorists would plant germ warfare weapons in places so far out of the way? If it was terrorists, why not London, New York, Moscow, Paris?"

"Too heavily protected?"

The Irishman held up his hand, flexed his index finger and hissed. "Aerosol. Doesn't take much."

"So it's nature," I say. "That's what these stories were getting at. Nature did this."

"Humankind's expansion *into* nature. Almost as if these plagues have always been there, a guard against us going too far. And when we did go too far…"

In one way it's a momentous idea that I can barely absorb. In another, more immediate way, it really does not matter.

I drift off to sleep thinking about the bomb in the channel tunnel, and how nature was far more subtle.

Next morning we eat a brief meal of tinned fruit then set off early. We want to reach Bar None today, if we're ever going to reach it at all.

We travel well that day, pausing here and there for one of the Range Rovers to push tangled cars from the road, stopping around lunchtime to refuel from the jerry cans in the back of the Irishman's vehicle.

We see more strange things, but try to ignore them.

Late afternoon we leave the motorway and head off across the countryside, following A-roads that twist between hills and valleys. These roads are generally quite clear, but when we come across the first real barrier, it's a bad one. An oil tanker has jack-knifed and exploded, taking a dozen cars with it, and we have to leave the road and drive through overgrown fields, skirting a few copses of trees that have strange growths at their centres, ploughing through hedges that grapple at wheels and axles. I take the rear, driving the bike along the route the Range Rovers are carving across the fields. I feel very vulnerable.

We make it back onto the road past the site of the accident, and head off once again in pursuit of a place that may not be.

But Bar None's existence is revealed to us long before we reach it.

I see her as we drive around a bend. She's standing in the middle of the road, away from any wrecked cars, wearing a white wedding dress over leather trousers and a leather jacket. The dress would probably fit her were it not for the clothes beneath, but it is bulged and stretched as though fit to burst. It's unnaturally clean. Her face is painted red.

I stop the bike and turn around. Jessica shrugs.

I look at the woman again and she's still standing there, smiling. She starts walking toward me. I rev the bike and drift forward another fifty metres, then kick down the stand and dismount.

I look around. To my left a steep hill rises away from the road, and to my right there are fields. There could be a hundred people hidden within a hundred steps of me, and I'd never see them. But I need to offer a peaceful sign to this woman, so I smile and walk to meet her. We both pause several steps from each other. There's something strange about her, way beyond the red-painted face and unusual attire, but I can't place it.

"We can't allow you to reach there," she says.

"Reach where?"

"Bar None."

We, she had said. Of course, I never believed she would have been on her own, but now I'm conscious of other eyes upon me. "Come with us," I say. That disarms her. She frowns, steps back, and that's when I realise what it is about her that's so strange. What I thought were loose threads from the hems of the wedding dress are in fact fine white roots, delving out from beneath the dress's sleeves, across the backs of her hands and around her fingers. There are some at her throat as well, fine white veins trailing upward for her face. The dress is unharmed. These are growing from beneath.

"You'd take me?" she whispers.

Now she's talking in the singular. If this is a game, I have to win. I can feel the others watching from inside the Range Rovers, and I step to one side to allow Jessica a clear shot.

"Have you not been there already?" I ask. The woman's face drops, all signs of hope slipping from the glazed paint. She spits, laughs, turns around to present her back to me.

"You think I'd have come out again if I had?"

"I don't know anything about Bar None," I say.

The woman spins around again, and spittle flies from her mouth. "Don't lie to me, fresh man. Don't fuck with the Wild Woman of Wongo. Last man who fucked with the Wild Woman left his dick inside. Shall I show you? Would you like to see?" She's lifting the wedding dress and hauling down the zipper on her trousers, and as she's distracted I take another look up at the hillside to my left. I can detect no movement there, but it's so overgrown that there could be anything hidden on its slopes.

"I don't need to see, I believe you," I say.

The woman lets her dress drop. "Oh, if you *did* see you'd *never* believe, fresh man. So innocent. So sheltered. Where have you been all my new life?"

I've no answer, and she spits again.

"Well, doesn't matter. You're not going there. We can't let you."

"Why not?"

"So you *do* know Bar None!"

I offer a rueful smile, as though she has won one over on me. "We just heard it's a nice place to stay."

"Nice?" She moves closer and now I can smell her, a mix of freshly cut grass, turned earth and raw meat. I glance down at her throat and see those roots stroking her chin, as though encouraging her to speak again. "Nice? It's nice if you like pain, and rot, and torture. Nice if you want your face flayed away and pebbles put in place of your eyes. *Then* it's nice, fresh man. Nice for you and all your fresh meat." She looks over my shoulder at the Range Rovers. She seems disappointed. "Fresh, but so sparse."

"We don't want trouble," I say. "We don't want anything from you, all we want to do is pass."

"Pass?"

"On the road. We just want to drive on."

She smiles, and her amazingly white teeth form a slash across her bloody red face. The laughter sounds real, and for a moment I think I can see the human being beneath this charade. I wonder what she was before the end, but realise that no longer matters. Might as well ask what she had been in a previous life. We are all reincarnated now, in this world that seems to carry so little of the past.

"I can't let you drive on," she says. "I'm hungry. My sweet pig-fucking God, I am so damn *hungry*."

Something happens to her teeth.

I turn, shout, run toward the motorbike, trip and fall to the ground. The shotgun breaks the air. Something strikes the road behind me. I scramble to my feet and run for the Range Rover, and it's as if the air is being torn around me, things whipping at my clothing, something cool and harsh slapping the back of my neck, and then the explosions come in and I realise someone is shooting at me. I hear thuds and other metallic sounds as I reach the lead Range Rover, then the shotgun sounds again, the air rifle snaps at the air, and I leap into the rear seat even as the vehicles start moving.

"Keep down!" Jessica shouts. I look up at the back of her head and see it haloed by a shower of shattered glass. I sit up anyway, because I can't bear not being able to see. Jessica curses and punches at the obscured windscreen without slowing. It falls in on her, a million diamonds that pile onto her and Cordell's laps and scatter around their feet, and I just see a flash of white and red before the Range Rover bumps over something lying in the road.

"Was that my bike?"

"Already passed that," Jessica says.

More gunshots. Cordell thrusts the shotgun from his side window and fires at the hillside, but I can't see what he's shooting at. The car shakes as bullets strike it, and the door lining to my left erupts in pieces. I glance back and see the Irishman following. As he passes over the shape in the road it's mostly red.

"Get down, damn it!" Jessica shouts again.

"What the hell was that?" I say. "What was the point?"

"I heard what she was saying," Cordell says. He breaks the shotgun, trying to hunker down low in the seat as he pops in two fresh cartridges. "About Bar None." He sits ups again, gun resting on the sill of the shattered windscreen.

I realise that the gunfire has stopped. Something is growling in the Range Rover's engine, but there are no more bullets trying to tear us apart. I look back again and the Irishman is on our tail. There are some holes in his windscreen but it has not shattered. He smiles and gives the thumbs up, and I wave back.

"There was something wrong with her," I say.

"You can fucking say that again!" Jessica says.

"No, I mean something that's not wrong with us."

"Yeah, well." Cordell leans forward and scans the road ahead, the hillside to our left, the tall, wide hedge that now borders the fields to our right. We round a bend and there's a bus parked beside the road, a car buried in its rear. Jessica presses down on the gas and we roar by, Cordell tracking the bus with the shotgun.

"So what was it?" Jessica says.

Cordell snorts. "Does it matter?"

"Weird," I say, "like she had something growing—"

The shotgun explodes and a spread of shrubs to our left coughs leaves. "Thought I saw something," Cordell says.

Jessica glances at me in the rear-view mirror.

"Maybe we can talk about this later," I say. It's noisy.

Wind whistles through where the windscreen had been, and I can see that Jessica and Cordell both have dozens of tiny cuts on their faces. Some of them drip blood, and I'm reminded of the red-faced woman we just left behind.

Jessica ran her over. I wonder whether it was on purpose, or because the road was not wide enough to avoid her. I try to remember where we had been standing, but I can't. I mourn the loss of the motorbike, a link to Michael, but I'm also strangely thrilled at what the red-faced woman had been saying. She and her friends knew of Bar None, which could only mean that it was real.

"We must be close," Cordell says.

"Why?"

"If they didn't want us to get there, they wouldn't be guarding roads miles away."

I dig around in the back of the Range Rover and find an old road atlas.

"Don't think we'll need that," Jessica says. Her eyes are stark against her blood-smeared face, and I realise for the first time how piercingly blue they are. Almost beautiful. I'd never thought of her that way before, and it surprises me.

I look back again to make sure the Irishman is still following. He seems fine, but this time he does not acknowledge my wave. He seems lost, in a world of his own. Daydreaming.

I close my eyes and a flood of images hits me. I recognise them, but at the same time I do not. They're not from my life.

"Has anyone…?" I begin, but trail off.

"What?" Jessica asks.

"Doesn't matter." I lie on the back seat and close my eyes, and this time I do not open them again. I don't sleep. But I do remember.

NINE

BLACK SHEEP

I'd been at the party for about half an hour, and already I believed this would be a night that would change my life.

I walked from room to room, carrying a bottle of Black Sheep in one hand and a spliff the size of a Cuban cigar in the other. I knew a few people here, but not many, and as was usual when I was drunk and stoned, it was those I did not know who interested me the most.

The house was big, befitting the status of its owner. Rufus was a record producer of some repute. Unfortunately his reputation came from being an unbearable cunt to everyone he worked with, and for investing most of his honestly-earned in various underground ventures. Some said his money reached as far as London's brothels, while others—probably under the influence of too much dope—suggested that the man was a major importer of drugs.

I just thought he was a prick, but he always threw a good party.

I took another draw on my spliff and put down the beer. I decided to make my way back out to the kitchen to liberate a bottle of wine from the fridge. I passed through the large open-plan space that incorporated the living room and dining area, nodding to a couple of people I knew and smiling at a couple of women who glanced my way. One of them looked away, the other smiled back, and I promised to come back to her once I had a drink.

In the corridor between the main room and kitchen I suddenly decided I needed a piss. I tried one door, which was locked, and when I opened the next door—bathroom, I was right—I stood back and smiled. Rufus was sitting on the edge of the bath being orally amused by two young ladies.

"Shut the fucking door!" he shouted. I nodded, took one more peek at the naked rumps facing my way, and clicked the door shut.

Obviously being a cunt had fringe benefits.

I stumbled back into the open-plan room, frowned, remembered that I'd been heading to the kitchen for a bottle of wine, and then I saw the woman I was going to marry.

That was it, right there. There are times in everyone's life when things change suddenly and irrevocably, and that was one of my main moments. She was standing close to the fireplace and smiling indulgently as a tall, seedy-looking man tried to impress her. She was holding an empty wine glass in her left hand, running her right index finger around its rim, and I swore I could hear the subtle hum coming off the glass. Above the loud music, shouts, laughter and banter, she was drawing me in.

I let her. I crossed the room, looking down as I stepped over splayed limbs and almost knocked over a drink, and when I looked up again she was staring right at me. I froze, and that was another moment. Our gazes locked and for a while we could not let go. The guy with her turned to stare at me, and perhaps he sensed something of what had happened because he swore and walked away. I finished making my way over to the fireplace, and realised I didn't have a clue of what to say.

"I'm going to marry you," I said.

She raised her left eyebrow and pursed her lips, and a wave of sensual excitement pricked at every inch of my skin. She took the spliff from my hand and stubbed it out in an ashtray. "Don't need drugs," she said.

"Me neither."

"What's your name?"

"A secret."

She raised that eyebrow again. Lifted her wine glass. "Refill?"

"I was just thinking the same thing."

We walked together, and when I touched her elbow it felt like the most natural thing in the world.

In the kitchen, everyone else around us now gone, all talk subdued, our own world expanding and begging to be filled with words and experience and history, I leaned in close and whispered my name in her ear.

"His name's Danny!" I sit up quickly, look back, and the Range Rover driven by the Irishman is buried in the hedge a few hundred yards behind us.

"Who?" Jessica asks.

"The Irishman's name is Danny," I say, and already I know that it's too late to stop.

Jessica slams on the brakes. Turns, looks over my shoulder at the crashed Range Rover. Cordell hefts the shotgun.

"Whatever his name, he's slipped from the road. Doesn't look too bad. If I reverse up and—"

"He's already dead," I say.

Jessica glares at me. "How can you know?"

Because I just had one of his memories, I think. But of course, I can't say that. Not at all. "I just do."

Something slaps against the vehicle's roof, then its wing, and the gunfire starts again. Jessica falls back into her seat and we skid away, slewing across the road before she brings us under control. "I wonder if they have transport," she says.

I wonder if they need it, I think.

"We can't just leave him," Cordell says. "We have to go back, get him out."

"No use," I say. "No point. I think he was shot during those first few seconds." His name was Danny, and he met the woman he was going to marry at a party thrown by a corrupt record producer. How could I know that? Why did it feel so much like a memory of my own, when it patently was not? I shake my head and shout as another bullet stars the side window.

"How can you be *sure?*" Jessica shouts.

"I saw him," I say, and though that really says nothing at all, she seems satisfied. She skids around the next corner and the shooting stops again.

The engine is making a rattling, low roar, and Jessica seems keen to get as far away as she can before it fails altogether. Then, I suppose we'll be on foot.

"How many cartridges do we have left?"

"A handful," Cordell says. He passes me the air rifle from between his feet, along with a tin of pellets.

"Might as well fart at them."

"It's better than nothing," he says.

I pump the air rifle and load it.

Something breaks, the vehicle judders, and Jessica just manages to coast to the top of a hill before the engine gives out with a bellow of smoke. She slips into neutral and we start rolling, and in the distance, between the slopes of two hills, I can see the sea.

"I think maybe we're almost there," I say.

"Up there! What the hell? What the *fuck?*" Cordell is pointing to our left. For a second I can't see what he's pointing at. An open field, the beginnings of a forest, nothing that seems to be a threat.

"What? Where?"

"In the trees!" He props the shotgun on the side door sill and fires. Even though I saw it coming the shot shocks me, and I close my eyes against the explosion. When I open them again I look up, through the haze of smoke being wafted quickly through the vehicle, and see what he has seen.

There are things in the trees. Between them, among them, and high in their canopies, all of them moving parallel to us, moving *strangely*.

"What *is* that?"

One of the figures flashes and a bullet hits the Range

Rover a few inches below my face.

Cordell fires again. I knock out my pocked side window and fire as well, though with the power of this air rifle and the distance involved, I may as well blow kisses.

"They're people," he says, breaking and reloading the shotgun. "But…"

"Changed," I say. I remember the red-faced woman and the roots curved around her hand, up her throat. There must have been much more hidden away beneath her clothing.

"How many of them?" Jessica asks.

I try to count, but it's difficult. "Lots. Why?"

"Because we'll be at the bottom of this hill in seconds." She tries bump-starting the Range Rover, but another cough of smoke from the engine says everything.

"Bar None must be around here somewhere."

"Why must it?"

"Because of them!" I point my gun from the window, shooting blind. "They're here because of it, trying to stop people from getting there. I don't know. They're the factions he told us about, the ones that don't agree. It just has to be, because if it isn't then we'll never reach it, and that's not the way this should end."

"What, you're talking fairness?" Cordell laughs.

I look up and see that the shapes have left the trees. They're running downhill toward us, closing in quickly, and they're moving faster than anyone I've ever seen before. I'm not quite sure exactly what I'm seeing—my brain has difficulty translating the images. There are faces and mouths, leaves and twigs, blooming flowers and bulbous tubers, and other things linking, entering or entwining everything else. Some of them pace, some of them roll. Others seem to float. More gunshots. The bullets go wide, and I think, *Surely they don't even need the guns anymore?*

"Holy shit," Jessica says.

"Yeah." I aim and fire the air rifle again. I'm sure I shot straight, but the thing I aimed at keeps on coming. He, she or it carries a shotgun, and they pepper the side of the Range Rover as they leap the tattered fence beside the road.

"Cordell!" I shout. He fires and the thing's shoulder explodes in a shower of feathered seedlings.

"No, I mean *holy shit!*" Jessica says. "Look. *Look!*"

As the vehicle drifts to a halt, the front grille nudges against a stone wall. Beyond the wall, a garden. Facing the garden, a couple of hundred metres away, is a large stone building.

"Do you think…?" I say.

"See him? Sitting on a garden bench?"

And I *can* see him, Michael, nursing a pint of beer and shielding his eyes from the sun as he watches us. He waves, then gestures us to him.

"Through the windscreen!" Cordell says. He fires the shotgun one more time then climbs from his seat, sliding across the bonnet and rolling over the head of the wall. When he stands and turns, a grin of amazement lights his face. He's looking straight at me, but through me as well. He drops the shotgun just as one of the strange people strikes the side of the vehicle, reaching in with bare barked fists to clasp my wrists. I prise them away, kick out at the thing's face, and Jessica helps me over the front seats. We exit the windscreen together. I feel the hot metal of the bonnet, then the cool stone wall, then the caress of soft grass as I drop to the ground.

Then I stand up, and look back, and see what Cordell saw.

"Welcome to Bar None," Michael says.

I'm so full of questions that I cannot speak. Cordell and Jessica are similarly stunned, by what we have come through and what we have seen; the deaths of Jacqueline and the Irishman, and our arrival at a place we thought might never exist. So many questions, so much left to know, and Michael smiling at us from the wooden bench, a half-full pint in his hand.

"Thanks," Jessica says.

I nod at Michael, then look up at the large building behind him. It's everyone's idea of a quaint country pub. There's ivy climbing toward the eaves, leaded windows, bare, random stone walls, a tiled roof with a chimney breathing smoke, and a sign hanging above the door with "Bar None" painted in extravagant white lettering. The picture below the name shows an approximation of the building set against a wide green background. It doesn't look quite right. Nothing about this place does, even though it's a cliché brought to life. Not quite right.

"What's inside?" I ask.

Michael laughs. "A pub, of course. But it's bigger than it looks. There are plenty of rooms, and many bars. Lots of places to sit and chat. And when you're ready, just follow the stairs up to your rooms."

"It doesn't look that big," Cordell says. Michael raises his glass and takes a drink.

"How did you get here before us?" Jessica asks.

"What were those people? Where have they gone?"

"Why were they trying to stop us coming in?"

The questions flood out, Cordell, Jessica and I stumbling over each other to ask what is on our minds. Michael lets us blabber on for a moment, then raises his free hand until we quieten.

"Please," he says, "there really is plenty of time. Go inside. Get yourself a drink and something to eat. It's on the house." He says no more, and when I go to ask another question he raises the glass to his lips and looks away.

I look at Cordell and Jessica, shrug, and I am the first one through the door.

The bar we enter is small and surprisingly bare. But it feels familiar, with a fire roaring in the fireplace, empty picture frames hanging haphazardly on the stone walls, and built-in benches and tables polished smooth by decades, perhaps centuries of custom. Some of the chairs have threadbare cushions, and few of them match. It smells of spilled beer and cooking, and all the sounds I associate with a good pub are here. All of them. Even the voices.

There are a dozen people sitting around the large room. A few of them are alone, drinking in contemplative silence. Others sit in pairs, chatting, laughing, seemingly without a care in the world. Eyes turn toward us then away again, unconcerned at our arrival. The oldest person must be in his nineties. The youngest, barely out of her teens.

"What can I get you?" The barman is a big man, with a bushy beard and strong hands resting atop his bar. He rearranges bar towels without looking, smiling at us as he awaits our order.

"How long have you—" Cordell begins, but I cut in.

"I'll have a Reverend James," I say. "And can we see your menu? Michael told us it's on the house."

The barman laughs as he takes down a pint glass from a hook above his head. "On the house! It is, that's true. Everything's on the house." He looks at Cordell and Jessica as he pours my pint. I can smell it, hear it flowing into the glass, and I wonder what memories will come to me tonight. I hope they will be my own.

Jessica and Cordell order drinks, we select some food, and the barman says he will bring it out to us. He assumes we are going back outside.

Michael is waiting for us, his glass now almost empty.

"Can I get you a refill?" I ask.

He shakes his head. "I think you'll all be listening, and I'll be talking, so perhaps after we're done. But thanks."

We sit down, and within minutes the barman appears with our food. It must have been ready on the plate for him to have brought it so quickly. I sniff my steak and ale pie suspiciously, but when I cut into it, watch the gravy ooze, feel the springy welcome of a mushroom beneath my knife, inhale the aroma...I know it will be heavenly.

"Heavenly," I say, and I begin to eat.

"Not quite," Michael says. "But let me explain. Then I'll let you all decide."

"I suspect you're wondering about the view. It's real, or as real as can be. It's the world as it will be when it's moved on. As it is now it's… clumsy. And sometimes messy. I think you saw that on the way here, and met some of the mess outside the grounds of Bar None. That's only temporary. It's a confusion of things, but they'll work themselves out."

"Into that?" I ask, pointing out beyond the wall.

"Into that."

Hungry as I am, I put down my fork and stare beyond the stone wall again. I have seen many images on TV and in books of how prehistory might have looked. Towering trees, exotic undergrowth, palms and ferns the size of a jetliner's wing, vines as thick as a man's leg, flowers blooming in innocent splendour and cacti the likes of which few could imagine. But these had only been images, painted or computer-generated. They had never been the real thing. This time I can really see, and hear the swish of a breeze through the high canopy, and smell the freshness of plants untouched by pollution and unsullied by humankind's thoughts of arrangement. I am looking at true, unimagined wilderness.

There are no birds or other animals. Perhaps they will come later.

"If it's not really there, how come we're seeing it?" Cordell asks.

"Because you need to. It'll help you to decide."

"Decide what?" Jessica asks, but I think we all know.

"Whether to stay or leave."

I take a swig of beer, close my eyes and sigh. I cut some more pie and eat it, luxuriating in the wonderful tastes and sensations, wishing this meal could last forever. "Well, we've been through so much to get here," I say.

"It's not as if we're going to leave now."

"Maybe," Michael says. "But you have time. A day and a night, spent here at Bar None. After then, the decision is yours."

"You make it sound like a trial," Jessica says.

"Trial period, maybe. But there's no prosecution, no defence. It's all up to you."

"Who are those other people inside?"

"More survivors."

"They've all decided?"

"Yes, all of them."

"No one decided to leave?"

Michael frowns. "To tell the truth, I can't remember. But I don't think so."

I finish my pie, glance around and then smile as I pick up the plate to lick it clean. Jessica and Cordell are equally enthused about their meals, and similarly keen to finish every scrap. I sit back on the bench and nurse the pint glass in my hand. It is half empty, or half full. Perhaps that was what Michael means when he says that we have to decide. If the glass is half empty then I will go out into this burgeoning new world, take my chances in the wilds. If it is half full then I will stay here, where food and drink were plentiful, and where...

"What do you want us to do?" I ask. "You know so much, you brought us here, but why? What do you want from us?"

"That's for you to decide. But first, another drink."

Michael stands and collects our glasses, takes them inside and leaves us out in the garden. The three of us are silent for a while, staring at the world beyond the low stone wall, trying to see where the Range Rover had come to rest but unable to make out anything manmade. I wonder whether it is even still there. If I cross back over that wall where will I be, and when? Will I enter the world I see now, or the one we left only half an hour before? So many questions that I cannot answer, and I suddenly feel vulnerable, unable to dictate my own fate and controlled so much by Michael. I am no longer even sure that he is a man.

"I have no idea what to do," Jessica says. I have never heard her sounding so weak and defeated. "I'm scared to stay, but even more frightened about leaving. We saw what it was like out there, and *that...*" She points at the wall, and the cliff of alien vegetation beyond. "*That's* nowhere to be."

Michael returns with a tray of fresh drinks. He sits beside me, with Jessica and Cordell on the bench opposite us, all four looking out across the well-kept pub garden to the stone wall and beyond.

"Bar None," I say. "You were going to tell us."

"I was," Michael says, and for an instant I am afraid that he has changed his mind.

But then he takes a long drink and smacks his lips, and I hear him whisper under his breath, "So, this is the last of them."

"The last of us?"

Jessica and Cordell look over. They hadn't heard Michael say that, only me.

"But what about those in there?" Jessica says. "And there must be other places like this, places where things are normal."

"Normal?" Michael runs his hand through his hair. "There is no normal. No middle ground. There can't be when there's such divergence, such deviation. Everyone is so different, no two people are the same, so how can there be normal?"

"Normal as in what we know," Cordell says.

"And what do you know? Very little. You've come this far for me, and I thank you for that. But can you explain your journey? Can you tell me what happened, and how, and why?"

I think of Jacqueline dying in the night and the Irishman (*Danny, his name was Danny*), those things in and above Newport, and being shot at by people who also had the attributes of plants.

"So where are we?" I ask.

"The last bar on Earth." Michael turns and raises his glass at the building behind us. "Yes, the last bar. The last place to get a good drink. Last place to sit before an open fire and talk about old times as if they really matter. And that's important, because they do. Old times matter *so much*. They're the geography of the present. They mark it and make it, setting out parameters and allowing certain things to be, and other things not to be."

"The past?"

"History. It's a living thing, and it needs to remain so. But there are factions that desire that this is not the case."

"You told us that before," I say. "So who are these factions?"

Michael looks at me, and I know instantly that I can never understand. "Groups. Belief systems. Gods of potential. They see history as something to be rid of, while others—me included—believe that it will always provide the foundation of the future."

"What about the present?" Cordell asks.

"That no longer exists. There's so much to either side of it—the rich past, the endless future—that this present is losing clarity and significance."

"So why are we here?" Jessica asks. "If certain factions don't want this place to be here, why are *we* here?"

"To protect the past," Michael says, "while you yourselves are protected."

We fall silent, trying to digest and understand but knowing that we probably never will. Time is becoming strange, and already I am sleepy, ready to dream and remember so much more of Ashley.

The two of us sat in the middle of a forest, drinking Reverend James from a bottle, me watching as she undid the buttons of her blouse with a sly smile on her lips...

Observing through the crack between door and frame as Ashley wasted another pregnancy test kit, negative, negative, and feeling ashamed at seeing tears meant only for herself...

Sat on the river boat with a hundred other tourists, the city of York flowing by as the silence built terribly between us, turning from a lack of anything to say to something too solid to ever breach again...

"Dreaming?" Michael says, and I snap out of it.

"Just tired."

"Then go to sleep. You each have a room. And in the morning we can talk some more."

"I have so many questions," Cordell says. "I don't think

I can sleep, and I'm not sure I trust this place."

"In the morning you'll have fewer questions. I promise."
Michael stands to leave.

"Wait!" I say.

"The morning."

"Where are you going?" Jessica asks.

Michael has started walking across the grass toward
the stone wall. He turns back and looks at all three of
us, touching us individually. "Guard duty."

We finish our drinks and go back inside. There are still
people scattered around the bar but I don't recognise
any of them, as though they have all changed positions
since I was last in here an hour before. The barman is
there, cheery and round, and he does his best to set us
at ease.

"Your rooms?" he asks.

I'm going to shake my head, demand answers, but
tiredness flushes through me again and I nod.

"There's hot running water, tea and coffee, fluffy towels
and fresh beds."

"No Sky TV?" Cordell asks.

"Forgot to renew our licence." He gestures around the
side of the bar and I see a door there, opening onto a
narrow staircase that climbs around a sharp curve.

"Which rooms are ours?" I ask.

"You'll know." He nods, then turns to serve another
customer.

"'We'll know,'" Jessica mimics quietly. "He's about as
fucking enigmatic as Michael."

But he's right. When we reach the top of the narrow

staircase the corridor opens out before us, heading in two directions and disappearing into an impossible distance. The carpet is thick but faded, the walls textured with bare painted plaster that looks as though it's half a millennium old. There are doors at regular intervals, bare wood polished by centuries of pushing hands, brass ironmongery equally shined. How many thousands of hands have connected with these handles, skin smeared with the remnants of a meal, or blood, or the sweat from a lover's thighs? Oddly, I decide, perhaps not many. Because although this place looks old, it feels new. It feels… unwalked. Most of the lights work, though a few are out, and picture frames containing nothing hang at random intervals. Bare wall. Not even any backing. It's as if the frames are presenting splinters of Bar None for our perusal.

More corridors lead left and right, and there are more staircases heading up and down. We climb one because it feels right and we're in another corridor, doors every dozen paces, all of them closed. I hear murmurs, whispers and an occasional cry.

"Bad dreams?" Jessica says.

"Maybe."

"The building isn't anywhere near this big," Cordell says.

"I'm so tired. I'm too tired to care. I just want to sleep." We walk on and then I see my room. The other two seem unconcerned when I open a door and step away from them, but it is so obviously my room that I can't do anything else. I have never been here before—I don't recognise the bed, the room's layout, the black oak beams piercing the ceiling or the patterned bedspread—but it welcomes me in, and I relax on the bed with absolutely no feelings of being displaced. On a table beside the bed rests a fresh pint of Reverend James. I sip.

Will I ever see Jessica and Cordell again? I think.

There's an en-suite bathroom, and for a few seconds I expect Ashley to open the door and emerge, smiling, welcoming me into my own private Heaven. But I check out the bathroom and return to the bed alone. As I slip away, I know that this place is nowhere close to paradise.

TEN

REBELLION

And there we were, sitting in the Mad Bear and Bishop on Paddington train station, me nursing a pint of Redruth Cornish Rebellion—orange and brown, good head, but with a stale tea aftertaste—and Ashley working her way through an expensive bottle of cheap red wine. I'd already finished one pint, but the pleasant alcohol fuzz was doing little to calm my nerves.

We had just taken the most momentous decision of our lives.

"Do you hate me?" Ashley asked.

"No, of course not." I wished I could make her believe, communicate with her mind-to-mind instead of only with words.

"You *must* hate me." She drained her glass and sighed, wiping her hand across the back of her mouth. It was a noisy pub—train announcements, chatting commuters, business people prattling into mobile phones—but I heard the sound her hand made across her lips. Her lips were already stained a dark violet from the wine, and I imagined kissing them. But now was not the time.

"I don't," I said. "Not in the slightest. I love you more because you can make a decision like that."

"But it should be our decision."

"It is!"

"But you said you wanted it so much."

I reached out and held her hand, pulling it across the table toward me. I hated the resistance I felt there, even though I knew it was because she was so unsure.

"And so did you," I said. "But sometimes it's not meant to be."

We had been to Harley Street to see a fertility specialist. She had revealed that no matter what we tried—fertility treatment, IVF—we would never have children. *I can't adopt*, Ashley had said as soon as we left the clinic, and it was the sudden, certain answer to a question we had both been musing upon for over a year.

I would have adopted. No question. But Ashley had made up her mind, and I loved her so much that I had no trouble respecting that.

"So it's just you and me," she said. She started crying, leaning in close so that she did not have to raise her voice. "Just you and me always, the two of us on holiday. No kids running around and getting lost and jumping in the pool. No screaming babies to wake us in the night. Nothing like that. No first day at school, no swimming certificates, no first words, no first smiles, no teenager problems. We'll never see our children marry. We'll never…" She sobbed, a violent cough that shook her shoulders and released a flood of tears. She could hardly speak to finish her sentence, but she had to. "We'll never… have… grandchildren."

I cried too, because I was not ashamed. A few heads turned but looked away again, allowing us the privacy of a crowd. Nobody asked us what was wrong because nobody really cared. Everyone here was going somewhere else—home to their partners and children, or home from their lovers—and the crying couple would soon be forgotten by everyone but ourselves.

We held each other close until the time came for us to board our train. I picked up Ashley's wine bottle as we left, bundled together as if to protect each other from the outside. The physical contact continued as we walked downstairs and out onto the platform, checked our tickets, boarded the train. Even as we sat down we held hands, desperate not to let each other go because we were all we had left.

"More wine," Ashley whispered into my ear. She smiled and kissed my neck. We drank from the bottle, and when a businessman across the aisle cast a disapproving look I smiled and raised the bottle to him. Ashley giggled.

We pulled out of the station and lost ourselves amid the sparkling London evening. A few minutes into the journey the wine bottle was empty, and Ashley relinquished physical contact to buy some more from the buffet cart.

"Don't be long," I said. I watched her sway her way along the carriage, disappearing through the sliding doors.

The businessman made some vague noise of disapproval and rustled his newspaper. At first I ignored him, but then his air of superiority began to rankle. I stared at him until he glanced up, met my eyes, looked away.

"Problem?" I asked.

He shook his head, obviously perturbed that the subject of his disapproval had decided to answer back.

"Really, I'm not causing trouble, but what's your problem with my wife and I sharing a drink?"

He looked up again, put down his paper. "No real problem," he said. He had an expensive haircut and manicured nails. He still had his suit jacket on, even though the train was warm. I hated him.

"It didn't sound like that," I said. "Please, just keep your grunts and sniffs to yourself."

He picked up his paper again, dismissing me. "Well, it's no good example for kids, is it?"

I looked up and down the train. "I can't see any kids," I said. "And what do you know? What do you know about kids, and how they'd look at me, and what they'd see?"

He looked up again. "I have two of my own." And it was his tone—slow, each word enunciated as though he were talking to a dog—that really struck home with me.

"Well, you're lucky!" I said. "You're lucky you have two. We have none!" There was so much more to say, but I bit my lip and leaned back in the seat, turning my head so that I was looking from the window. Even then I could see the businessman's reflection. I was pleased to see that he'd lifted the paper to hide himself away entirely. *I have two of my own*, he'd said, as though he were superior, his kids more deserving of the air we were breathing than me. *I have two of my own.*

I cried, and when Ashley returned she sat beside me, opened the wine, and I never mentioned that man and our conversation to her, ever. We drank that bottle and I went to buy another. When I returned I looked for signs that Ashley and the man had been talking, but he seemed to have nodded off in his seat, and my beautiful wife was staring from the window as I had been earlier.

Drunk, emotional, so in love, we both laughed when the businessman shook himself awake to discover that he had missed his stop. At first he cursed, but then he smiled and laughed with us, and I felt a crippling weight of bitterness lift away from me before it had ever truly landed.

I wake in the middle of the night to hear someone screaming. For a second or two I'm disorientated; am I at home, in the mansion, at Bar None? Then I jump from the bed and stand motionless in the middle of my room, breathing lightly so as not to mask any sounds. The screaming has stopped, but I think I can hear sobbing coming from far away. It's not a pleasant sound, but I am unsure of it: maybe it's only the plumbing coming to life.

I feel the wetness of tears on my cheeks. My eyes are sore. I want to dream of Ashley again and again, but there was something about that last dream that felt so final. The closure of a life. And, perhaps, my acceptance of her death.

I go to the window and look out. My view is of the huge garden to the rear of Bar None, a place I have not seen before now. It's much like the front, except more expansive. Dozens of tables and chairs form octagonal shadows across the grass, planted seating areas are scattered here and there, and in the distance I can make out the skeleton of a children's playground. *Haven't seen any children*, I think, but that does not mean there are none. Those long corridors behind me, those hundreds of doors, stairs and ramps and hidden routes up and down... all far too large to be contained within such a building. Impossible. And yet, like last night, I don't find it difficult to accept.

Beyond the garden I see the shadow of mountainous undergrowth. I wonder if it's really there, or whether it's still just an image of what will be. *Perhaps I should go and see*. But it's dark out there, and I know it's dangerous. And my bed is calling me back.

Climbing beneath the covers I try to step back, disassociate myself from where I am so that I can take an objective view. But however fantastic and impossible Bar None is becoming, none of it feels like a surprise.

I think of Michael out there on guard duty, hoping that I never have to see what he's guarding against.

I drift off. Memories come in, and this time none of them are my own.

I watched my mother fading away from cancer. She was nowhere near the woman she used to be. She had lost weight, become vague, looking like a sad, distorted echo of her old self. She knew what was happening, and that was worse. She knew everything. Even as I sat there crying, she reached out a skeletal hand to calm me down.

"Come on, Son," she said. "Don't be so sad. You're a good boy. Don't be sad."

"But I don't want you to go," I said.

"Everyone has to go. This is my time. And I think maybe I'm having an easier escape than you." She meant the plagues, of course, and the troubles as countries across the world tried to take what they could from their dying neighbours. Living in the Outback we were somewhat removed, but even here the end was drawing near.

"Perhaps," I said. I did not tell her about the sores that had broken out across my chest. I had maybe a couple of weeks, she had a day or two. She did not need to know.

I held her hand, and we talked about old times.

***

Daddy put me on his shoulders. He always did that. He'd tickle my legs and pull my toes, and I always thought I was going to fall, but I never did, because Daddy was holding me and he'd never let me fall.

We walked along the canal to the wharf. We saw: a heron, a kingfisher, three ducks, two swans, about a million cows, a sparrow hawk, someone's old bike thrown in the canal, and a man running with a rucksack on his back. Daddy walked, said he couldn't run with me on his back because I was getting to be such a big girl. I know I was heavy, because his head got wet and sweaty. But he carried me all the way, just like he said he would.

When we got to the wharf Daddy sat by the canal and gave me two pounds to go to the shop and get a drink and some chocolate. I waited in the queue for a while and bought some water, and some chocolate biscuits which the lady said she'd baked that day. Daddy and me sat on a bench and watched the barges go by, and we ate our stuff and drank the water. We didn't speak much. I liked the quiet, and watching the water swirl and bubble behind the boats. Daddy stared across the water and through the trees, like he was trying to see his way back home.

"What's wrong?" I asked him.

"Nothing, sweetheart." He stroked my hair and tickled me under the chin.

"Is it what you saw on telly?" There'd been lots of people talking, and pictures of dead people piled up in the backs of lorries.

"That's a long way away," he said.

"It doesn't happen here?"

"No, it doesn't happen here."

"Like tornadoes and hurricanes and earthquakes. They don't happen here."

"No sweetie, they don't."

I drank some more water and watched a family of ducks waddle past us to the canal. "Wouldn't matter if they did," I said. "You'd look after me."

Daddy didn't say anything else. He just looked across the canal again, past the trees.

We were hunting deep in the woods, three days out from our village, when the explosion came. It shook the world. We fell, knocked down by the shockwave, shaken from our feet, down was up and up was down and we lost consciousness for a long time.

When we woke up the world had changed. Our clothes had been scorched from our bodies, out hair frazzled by fire. Trees had fallen all around us. Some of them were snapped off close to the ground, their trunks—thick as my waist—splintered like a twig in a child's hands. Others had been uprooted, literally torn from the ground. All around us was clear of fallen leaves, because they had all been blown away.

Leonid started to whisper. "Did you see? Did you see?"

I shook my head, unable to speak. I had seen *something*. I had heard *something*. But it was so far beyond my comprehension that I could barely speak of it. Years later, when the world began to take interest in what had happened, I tried. But not then.

"*I saw*," Leonid said.

In the distance a column of fire connected heaven and earth. Leonid and I huddled together, agreeing that it was still the middle of the night, and we watched to see what would happen next.

***

I stood there, even though I knew they would take me. I kept the bag in my hand. I waved. Perhaps they would drive on, but I thought not, I *hoped* not. They were a hundred tonnes of metal and I was me, but sometimes you just have to make a stand.

"Really," he said, "do you think he won't know?"

"He won't know. The bomb is in the document case. I'll slide it under the table, then leave, and soon it will all be over."

"Do you think this will work? Do you think it'll change anything?"

I shrugged, because doubt had already planted its tendrils in my mind. "Somebody has to try."

I wake up with the thoughts of people, places and times I don't know buzzing through my mind. They begin to fade as I wash and dress. As I draw the curtains and look out upon Bar None's back garden once again, I can barely recall who I was, or where, or when.

I open the door to my room and close it behind me. There's no key. I try to remember which way I had come last night. I look left and right. The views are almost the same: corridor, doors.

I hear the sound of someone crying. It comes from far away, and I have to tilt my head to catch it again. I wait until there's another sob and then follow, turning right, heading down a staircase that curls around a column of carved stone, along a long corridor, turning left, and finding myself back in the bar we had been in the previous evening.

It has the early morning feel of any pub. There are still a few empty glasses around, and the smell of stale cigarettes, and the bar top is clean and polished. The crying has gone, and the room is now spookily silent, like any quiet place that should be bustling. No sign of the barman or anyone else. The front door is closed, curtains drawn over the windows on either side, and for some reason I feel that I should wait for permission before opening them.

The crying comes again, seemingly further away than before. I frown. It's an intensely personal sound; someone sobbing through their grief.

Trying to shut the crying out, I pour myself a glass of orange juice from an open container on the bar. It still tastes good and fresh, and I wonder where Bar None gets its stock from. *Nowhere*, I think. *It's just here.* Strange.

Above the fireplace hang several picture frames. All but one are empty, framing only rectangles of bare wall. The one that is not empty contains a photograph of six people standing in front of the pub. It's obviously an old picture, I can tell that from their clothing, but the pub looks no different. If anything, it looks a little older. The sky is uniform, depthless and bland, but the plants and flowers visible in the picture are beautiful. Even though it's black and white, I can appreciate their lushness.

I look closer at the faces, certain that I will see myself. But they are all strangers to me.

I walk slowly around the bar, taking everything in and trying to make sense of things. There's a doorway I hadn't seen the night before, and the crying comes again, louder, issuing from this new opening. I put down my glass and enter, emerging into a long, narrow corridor that twists its way through a cave of roughly plastered walls. The sobbing is coming from ahead of me, interspersed with someone trying to catch their breath, and it's heartfelt and uncontrollable. There's something in the sobs that I recognise, some tone of voice, and I walk faster.

The corridor emerges into another bar. As I step through the crying stops, though there's an expectant feel to the place. *Am I intruding?* I wonder. *Should I just turn around and leave?* But something holds me here, a sense that I belong. And I want to help.

This bar is much larger than the first, consisting of an

island unit made of oak and polished brass, and dozens of low tables set at random around the room. There are three fireplaces, all of them still exuding heat from dead fires. It appears empty of people, but there are glasses and dirty plates on many of the low tables. Leather sofas, wooden bar stools, and dozens of picture frames hang at random all around the bar. Most of them are empty, but one or two hold images I suddenly need to see. I hurry across the room, dodging between tables, and as I approach one picture I know that I will not recognise it. It's a photograph of three people on Prince's Street in Edinburgh. One of them is in a wheelchair, arms raised and face bright with her smile.

Someone else's memory.

I look around for the crying person. "Hello?" I say, but there's no answer. I feel so alone.

The other frame contains a picture that is familiar: an unknown man sitting beside a canal, a little girl by his side. She's holding a buttercup beneath his chin, laughing. The man cannot bring himself to smile.

That's not me, but I know the scene. I've never been there, but I recognise the ivy-clad building behind them, the line of boats parked along the canal, the old stone boat sheds built into the hillside.

It's so familiar, yet painfully distant, like a dream I will never again recall.

The crying bursts in again, contained and now released, and I jump in surprise. Around the other side of the bar I see an old leather sofa, and Jessica is sitting there, holding a picture frame in her lap. On the wall behind her is a lighter patch from where the picture has been removed.

"Jessica?"

She looks at me and tries to smile, but the tears won't let her. Neither can she talk. She just cries, and looks down at the picture.

I go to her, ready to turn around and leave if that's what she wants. But she lets me sit beside her, slides the frame across to me, and buries her face in her hands.

The frame contains a photograph of a tall, handsome man standing with his hand on the shoulder of a young boy. They're in a long line of people, queuing in front of a hospital. The man has an ugly plague welt on his face. The boy is no more than four, but his eyes are instantly familiar.

"I never... wanted to believe," Jessica says. "Even now, even here, I thought... there'd be a chance. They were in France, with his mother. My *husband*. My *child*. I *refused* to believe. I drove grief down. Beat at it. Never allowed it in. It was just too terrible..."

I put the picture down between us. "But someone has remembered it for you," I say.

Jessica looks up at me, and I can see what this is doing to her. I've suffered for many months, ever since Ashley died. Jessica is suffering that much grief in one go.

"Jess," I say, but she holds out her hand as if to ward me back.

"My fault," she says. "You gave me the chance... so many times. Now I have to go through this...on my own."

"No," I say. "Not on your own."

She almost smiles, but the tears start flowing again. "To begin with, I do," she says.

I nod, stand and walk away. There are other doorways leading from here, other rooms, other bars, and I know that soon I will get to know them all. But for now I need something familiar.

Back in the first bar I replenish my orange juice, sit in a window seat and wait.

There's a bang at the front door, another, and then it bursts open and Michael falls in. He's wounded. Blood flows from several injuries on his face and scalp, and he's holding his left arm awkwardly across his chest.

"What happened?" I ask.

He looks at me, and for an instant his eyes go wide, frightened. Then he shuts the door behind him and relaxes against it. "You're not supposed to be up yet."

"Who says?"

"No one. It's just... well, things are still changing, obviously."

"Are you all right? What happened?"

"Bit of a rumble at the wall." He winces as he pushes himself from the door and approaches the bar.

"The factions that don't want change?"

Michael looks at me for a long time. I become increasingly uncomfortable beneath his examination, yet I do not look away. *Answers*, I think. *He owes me some, and he knows it. Maybe now, with me down here alone, him injured...*

"There have been talks," he says. "The change is accepted. Really, it always was. It's the way of things. What some factions can't accept is you and your friends."

"Us? What have we done?"

"You remember." He leans over the bar and grabs a couple of pint glasses.

"Bit early, isn't it?" I ask, but I am remembering the dying mother, the happy child disturbed by her unsettled father. People I do not know in places I have never been. All mine.

Michael pours the beers—First Gold—and hands me a glass. "Sit down," he says. "We need to talk."

We choose a place by the fireplace. It still radiates warmth, and there's something about an empty pub that always feels cool, however warm it really is. The beer tastes good. No, not good. *Perfect.*

"You remember things," he says.

"Yes. Ashley, and what happened to us."

"And other things."

I nod. "Stuff I shouldn't know."

"It's a story, a living history rather than one written in books. There's you, your two friends, and many others who have been brought here. But there are certain groups that believe the progression should be total, with no allowance for history. I can't believe that. I never have, and I never will."

"Progression?"

"The world moving on. Humanity will be wiped clean, but why should it be forgotten? It's part of the planet's story, after all. An important part, both good and bad. *Why should it be forgotten?*" He speaks as though he's trying to persuade me of things, when in reality I hardly understand.

"So what is Bar None?" I ask. "It's no place normal."

"As I've told you, it's the last bar on Earth. It's a real

place, just… changed. The last bar, the last place, and you…"

"We're the last people."

"Soon enough."

I take a drink, close my eyes to savour the taste. *The last people.*

"We're humanity's memory."

Michael nods. "Does that make you scared?"

"Yes. My own memories are painful enough."

"You'll be safe here. You'll be protected, and you can do what you want within these grounds."

"And the things—the factions—that don't want us here? They want us wiped out, right? Want humanity to be gone, with no memory?"

"You'll be protected from them."

I look at his arm, the blood still dripping from the cuts on his face. "For how long?"

"Always. But I have to ask you one thing. I have to ask *you* to decide."

"To stay or leave."

"Free will. I can't force you to stay here."

"Like a vampire, right? You need my permission to come into my head?"

Michael looks away.

"Free will. That's what God supposedly gave us."

He drinks.

I stand, finish my beer and place the glass gently on the table. "The door's open now?"

Michael nods hesitantly. He looks surprised. I like that, because it means he can't read me quite as well as he thinks. I may be human and he may be something else, but I still own myself.

Without looking at him again I open the door and go out into the front garden. I close the door behind me and breathe in the fresh air.

It's beautiful here. Plants I recognise, birds I know, the perfect garden of a perfect pub where all of humanity can be discussed and remembered over pints of perfect beer. Really, what more could I ask for right now?

I look beyond the garden at the wall of vegetation I cannot possibly know. There are things moving up there, maybe alive, maybe some part of the new species of plants. This is how things will soon be, Michael said, but there must come a point where what actually exists beyond the wall, and what I now see, are the same.

I decide to take a walk.

ELEVEN

FIRST COLD

I reach the wall where we fell into the garden the previous day. Past the wall I see only a jungle of new plants, with unknown shadows shifting here and there inside. For some reason I feel safe, even though this new place exudes a deadly malevolence. This is how things will be, not how they are. But really, what does that change? It's only a matter of time.

I climb onto the wall and step forward.

I land beside the Range Rover. It's a wreck, rusted and holed, as though it has been here forever.

The view before me changes instantly, back to something I can almost recognise. It's not normal by any means, but the road is still vaguely visible, and I can see stone walls dividing fields, hedgerows planted by hopeful farmers, gates and fences that are already smothered with rampant growth.

And ahead of me, a few dozen footsteps away, the things

that had run at us from the hillside, shooting and killing Danny the Irishman in the process. They have taken root. They were once people, perhaps, but now their arms and legs have stretched, thickening into gnarled branches and fresh shoots. They scream when they see me. I scream back, shock and terror pushing me back against the stone.

The first of them reaches with impossibly long arms, clacking twigs together and rumbling in its chest. A chuckle? Hunger? I cannot stay to find out.

I lift myself up and roll back, tumbling to the ground behind the wall once more. For an instant I hear the gruff chuckling continue, but then it fades and is replaced once again by the sounds and smells of what will be.

My heart is racing, and I think I'm going to be sick. But there is a spread of bluebells around me—flowers I know and love—and suddenly I realise that this bluebell spring will not be my last.

"We're both staying," Cordell says. Jessica is beside him on the bench. Her face is red and puffy, her eyes distant, but she still gives me a small nod. That means a lot.

I sit opposite, glancing back at the wall.

"What did you see?" Cordell asks.

"Things changing. Has Michael spoken to you?"

"Yes, both of us."

I nod. "Good. Good."

Cordell drains his pint. "So what now?"

I smile, pick up his glass and stand. "What's yours?"

Night Shade Books Is an Independent Publisher of Quality SF, Fantasy and Horror

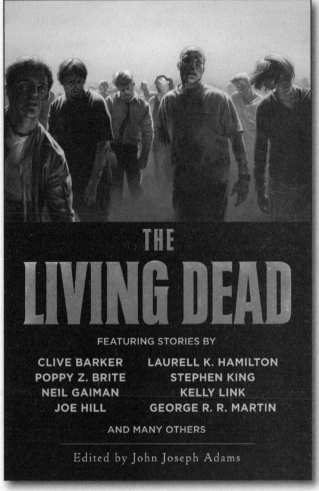

THE LIVING DEAD

FEATURING STORIES BY

CLIVE BARKER	LAURELL K. HAMILTON
POPPY Z. BRITE	STEPHEN KING
NEIL GAIMAN	KELLY LINK
JOE HILL	GEORGE R. R. MARTIN

AND MANY OTHERS

Edited by John Joseph Adams

ISBN 978-1-59780-143-0, Trade Paperback; $15.95

From *White Zombie* to *Dawn of the Dead*; from *Resident Evil* to *World War Z*, zombies have invaded popular culture, becoming the monsters that best express the fears and anxieties of the modern west.

Gathering together the best zombie literature of the last three decades from many of today's most renowned authors of fantasy, speculative fiction, and horror, *The Living Dead* covers the broad spectrum of zombie fiction; from Romero-style zombies to reanimated corpses to voodoo zombies and beyond.

Night Shade Books Is an Independent Publisher of Quality SF, Fantasy and Horror

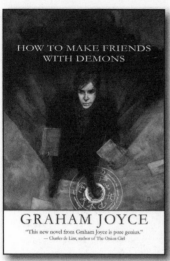

ISBN: 978-1-59780-142-3
Hardcover; $24.95

William Heaney is a man well acquainted with demons. Not his broken family - his wife has left him for a celebrity chef, his snobbish teenaged son despises him, and his daughter's new boyfriend resembles Nosferatu - nor his drinking problem, nor his unfulfilling government job, but real demons.

For demons are real, and William has identified one thousand five hundred and sixty-seven smoky figures, dwelling on the shadowy fringes of human life, influencing our decisions with their sweet and poisoned voices.

ISBN 978-1-59780-127-0
Trade Paperback; $13.95

College student Laura Harker was saved from a fate worse than death at the hands (and fangs) of a centuries-old vampire priestess and her Satanic minions. Her rescuer, an awkward, geeky folklore student named Teddy, single-handedly slew the undead occupants of the Omega Alpha sorority house, spurred into heroic action by fate itself, inexorably intertwining his and Laura's destinies.

A decade later, Ted stumbles onto a group of Cthulhu cultists planning to awaken the Old Ones through mystic incantations culled from the fabled Necronomicon. He and Laura must prevent an innocent shopping center from turning into... *The Mall of Cthulhu.*

Find these Night Shade titles and many others online at http://www.nightshadebooks.com or wherever books are sold.

Night Shade Books Is an Independent Publisher of Quality SF, Fantasy and Horror

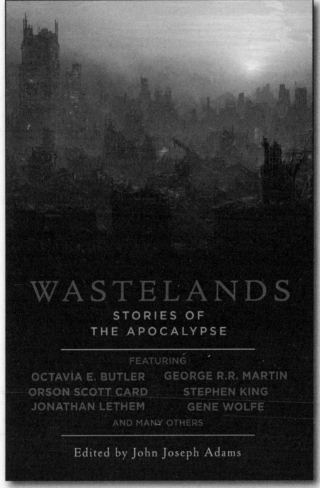

WASTELANDS
STORIES OF
THE APOCALYPSE

FEATURING

OCTAVIA E. BUTLER   GEORGE R.R. MARTIN
ORSON SCOTT CARD   STEPHEN KING
JONATHAN LETHEM   GENE WOLFE
AND MANY OTHERS

Edited by John Joseph Adams

ISBN 978-1-59780-105-8, Trade Paperback; $15.95

Famine, Death, War, and Pestilence: The Four Horsemen of the Apocalypse, the harbingers of Armageddon - these are our guides through the Wastelands

From the *Book of Revelations* to *The Road Warrior;* from *A Canticle for Leibowitz* to *The Road,* storytellers have long imagined the end of the world, weaving eschatological tales of catastrophe, chaos, and calamity. In doing so, these visionary authors have addressed one of the most challenging and enduring themes of imaginative fiction: the nature of life in the aftermath of total societal collapse.

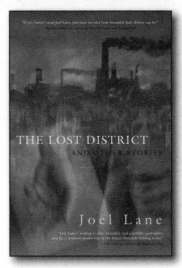

Night Shade Books Is an Independent Publisher of Quality SF, Fantasy and Horror

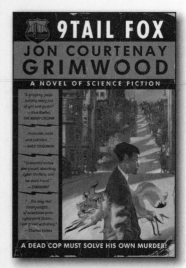

Night Shade Books Is an Independent Publisher of Quality SF, Fantasy and Horror

High fashion, corporate malfeasance, celebrity culture, and an obsessed media collide with exuberant violence and volatile intensity in the explosive debut cyberpunk thriller by newcomer Jon Armstrong.

When an assassin's bullets pierce Michael's body before the unblinking eyes of cameras, reporters, and viewers at a press junket, everything changes, forcing Michael to question everything about his previously perfect world.

ISBN: 978-1-59780-065-5
Trade Papberback; $14.95

Narcoleptic Adam Buckley is sleeping through his life. He sees people at parties he doesn't remember meeting, but who know him. Deep in London's sprawling Underground, he sees shadows figures beckoning him into tunnels not on any map. As Adam tries to find the secret to his own memories beneath the city, he realizes he is not alone.

A madman has taken to pushing people onto the tracks, and it may be someone Adam knows. If only he can remember, before it is too late... Suggestions of half remembered life, and the encroaching threat of violence begins to engulf him, and everyone he knows.

ISBN 978-1-59780-075-4
Trade Paperback; $13.95

Find these Night Shade titles and many others online at http://www.nightshadebooks.com or wherever books are sold.

Tim Lebbon's first published story was in the UK indie magazine *Psychotrope* in 1994, and in 1997 Tanjen published his first novel *Mesmer*. Since then he has had over thirty books published in the UK and US. He has won the Stoker Award and the British Fantasy Award multiple times – most recently for his novel *Dusk*, and been nominated for the prestigious World Fantasy and IHG awards.

He was born in London in 1969, lived in Devon until he was eight, and the next twenty years were spent in Newport. He and his wife Tracey now live in the little village of Goytre in Monmouthshire with their children Ellie and Daniel.

Tim can be found online at www.timlebbon.net